ALI *and* SILVANA

Also by Bob and Barbara Hitching
Nejla

ALI and SILVANA

Bob & Barbara Hitching

STL Books

PO Box 48, Bromley, Kent, England
PO Box 28, Waynesboro, Georgia, USA
PO Box 656, Bombay 1, India

© 1987 Bob and Barbara Hitching

First published 1987

STL Books are published by Send The Light (Operation Mobilisation), PO Box 48, Bromley, Kent, England.

British Library Cataloguing in Publication Data
Hitching, Bob
    Ali and Silvana
    I. Title
    823'.914[F]   PR6058.I8

    ISBN 1 85078 023 4

Typesetting, production and printing by
Nuprint Ltd, Harpenden, Herts AL5 4SE.

Dedicated to Eugene Pushkov
who, because of his obedience to God,
today experiences the agony of separation
from his loved ones.

CONTENTS

1	Ali	11
2	The News	14
3	Father Dimitri	20
4	The Telephone Call	26
5	Together	30
6	The Letter	35
7	Mavramati	41
8	Costas	51
9	Aysha	57
10	The Holy Book	61
11	New Friends	68
12	The Party	74
13	Wedding Day	80
14	Insights	94
15	Questions	102
16	The Dream	108
17	The Valley of Death	117
18	Freedom	123
19	Answers	129

20	Plans	134
21	The Uncles	136
22	Mehmet's Revenge	141
23	Beyond the Grave	147
24	Silvana's Gift	150
25	The Promise of Spring	156
	From the authors	159

ACKNOWLEDGEMENTS

We are deeply grateful to Paul and Connie Beals, who provided a cottage in the mountains where we worked on this book; to Ellen Hovis, who sat with a typewriter on her lap as we travelled across Europe; to Krista Clark, who plodded patiently through reams of paper until we had the final manuscript; and also to Ruth March, our editor who has become our friend.

1

Ali

Ali looked across the sparkling water to the island on the horizon. It was a clear day and he could just make out the outline of the far-away little houses with their brownish-red tiled roofs. To come to this place was always a joy for him. It provided a retreat from the pressures of his studies; a relief from the sense of always having to perform for his family and friends in the way they expected.

Today, he was preoccupied with thoughts of Silvana. His heart warmed towards her, but there were feelings almost of tragedy there as well. If only she were not a Christian!

Picking up a twig, he sat on the fresh green hill, and began to scratch in the soil; idly, without conscious thought. When he looked at what he had carved into the earth, and saw the letters 'S-I-L-V', he smiled, and then tossed the twig away.

Earlier that day, he had almost come to the point of telling his mother about Silvana. He had walked into the kitchen, taken a deep breath and had just been about to speak, when his cousin, Aysha, had popped her head around the door. It was not that he did not like Aysha. In fact, out of all the family, she would probably be the one who would understand best.

But he had felt too shy to speak about his private feelings in front of her, and so had excused himself and had come, at last, here; to his favourite spot on the hills overlooking the sea.

He thought back to that evening when he and Silvana had walked and talked for hours on end. The rain had suddenly poured down and they had laughed, enjoying its freshness. He remembered looking into her face that was so fresh and kind, her large brown eyes that were so innocent. Her hair, dripping wet, had clung flatly to the side of her face and neck. In the sudden intensity, the words 'Silvana, I love you' had just tumbled from his lips. Her reaction had been stunned; but after a short moment of silence, she had looked up, and shyly whispered, 'Ali, I love you too.' He could still remember that sense of awesome warmth, with a tingling that had surged throughout his soul. Yet now, as he looked across to the island, he could only feel a terrible sense of frustration and helplessness. They were both caught up in a system that was impossible to break. Even the history books were a constant reminder that their futures were destined never to be linked.

The call to prayer came resounding across the hill from the nearby mosque. He looked away, almost defiantly. 'Surely,' he thought, 'God would not want people like Silvana and myself to suffer just because of people's petty religious ideas? But no,' he realised suddenly, 'they aren't petty. Those ideas are really quite enormous. They have grown into this all-encompassing, growing prejudice so deep that the love of two young people could quite easily be sacrificed, just to sustain the system.'

He kicked the ground in anger and then shouted, 'Silvana, I love you!' The empty silence seemed to mock him. In despair, he bowed his head in his hands and, groaning, whispered, 'I want you to be my wife. Oh, why should we have to submit to the whims of fate?'

2

The News

The crowded street pulsated with life. Melina wore a brightly coloured dress, which fitted in well with the sea of colours and motion around her. Her long brown hair hung loose, and blew with the breeze. Melina loved the market. There was always an air of excitement about it, but also the comfortable security of familiar, everyday life.

A passerby would not have classified Melina as beautiful. She was slender and of medium height. Her face was ordinary, but her beautiful, expressive eyes were outstanding. They always seemed to portray her feelings, and right now they sparkled and seemed to dance as she looked about her.

Sitting cross-legged in a little bazaar stall was an enormously fat man. He wore a woolly hat that made him look almost spherical. In his hand was a glass of tea, and his beady eyes darted back and forth as he shouted comments to potential customers passing by. 'Come in and see,' he cried. 'Come in and see!'

For a moment, Melina stopped and looked at what was going on. Nobody was taking any notice of him; it was almost as if they couldn't hear him, and yet the volume of his voice was certainly great enough. She saw the funny side of the situation and smiled. As she turned to walk down one of the smaller streets, somebody grabbed her by the arm.

'Melina!'

'Silvana!' Melina's momentary panic evaporated into pleasure as she recognised her friend. 'It's lovely to see you. I didn't know you were back – I thought you were still away at college.'

'Oh...' Silvana looked away, her voice suddenly evasive. 'I came home to help out for a while. Mother has been terribly ill.'

Melina and Silvana had known each other as long as they could remember. Their parents were close friends, they had lived close to each other, and attended the same school.

'I hadn't heard that your mother was ill,' said Melina, feeling concerned. 'Is she getting better now?'

'A little, but it has been so worrying.'

Silvana was short and wore her black hair pulled back away from her face. She had fair skin, which contrasted with her dark hair and gave her an appearance of fragility. Her features were dainty and attractive. Right now, however, her face seemed tense and drawn, and there was not the normal exuberance in her step.

Melina sympathetically slipped her arm about her friend's waist. 'Let's go back to my house and we can talk.'

'Good.' Silvana seemed relieved to see Melina and was happy to go with her.

The little room was warm and friendly. There was an abundance of plants; some hung from the ceiling in little wicker baskets and others were neatly arranged along the various shelves and ledges. There were the customary family photographs scattered around the walls; some in neat frames, and other, smaller prints were tucked into the inside corners of the larger frames, with their ends slowly becoming bent with age. Overall, the room emanated an atmosphere that was cosy and relaxing.

'Let me get you some coffee. Do you still take it without sugar?' Melina left the room and went into the kitchen. Silvana looked around and, feeling quite at home, slouched down in the chair, beginning to feel some of the tension drain away. She was grateful for this dear friend.

'What's college like?'

Melina had reappeared, holding a tray with coffee and the usual overflowing plate of cookies and cakes. The sun tumbled through the window and shone on her hair, giving it a slight coppery tint and causing it to gleam.

'It's fine, but I find it difficult not knowing many people there. It's so casual in the way people behave, I'm not used to it.' Silvana looked unhappy at the subject of college, and Melina's concern was re-awakened.

'May I come around and help with your mother? I'm sure you must be tired.'

'No!' Silvana jumped up. Agitated, she crossed the room, took a book off the shelf and, flipping through the pages, tried to regain her composure.

'Is this book new? I've not seen it before.'

'Silvana, what is wrong?' asked Melina, now seriously worried. 'Why are you so upset?'

Silvana turned round, her face stricken. 'Oh Melina,' she began, 'I, I . . .', then she broke down, weeping.

Melina quickly moved across the room and put her arm around her friend, leading her like a child to the couch. Sensing that words were inadequate, she just sat with her arm gently around Silvana's shoulder.

When the sobs subsided, Silvana looked up shyly. 'Melina, I lied to you. I'm sorry. Mother isn't ill, it was the only thing I could think of at the time.'

'That's all right, you obviously have something weighing on your mind.' She reached over and held her friend's hand. 'Do you want to tell me about it?'

'I'm in love.'

'But that's wonderful! Why should that make you so sad?'

Silvana slowly breathed in, sighed, and tilting her head she looked, almost defiantly, into Melina's eyes.

'He is a Muslim.'

'Oh, no – !' With horror Melina dropped her friend's hand. A wave of nausea swept over her, quickly followed by a flush of anger.

'Silv, you must be mad!' Melina jumped to her feet and pointed an accusing finger at her friend. She was shouting angrily, and for a moment her mind flashed back to the man in the marketplace; shouting, completely unheard.

'Have you never read your history books? Have you never heard your grandmother's stories? I don't

have a grandmother and you know the reason why.'
Reaching over, she grasped Silvana by the shoulders,
shaking her with rage. Tears pouring down her
cheeks, she shouted almost hysterically, 'Shall I tell
you again why I have no grandmother?'

'Stop! Please, Melina, stop it!'

'Shall I give you the gory details how those
Muslims . . . ?'

'Stop!' Silvana screamed, as she broke loose from
Melina's grasp. Her eyes blinded by tears, she ran
stumbling out of the house.

Melina stood, as if frozen, with her hands out-
stretched in a lifeless manner, shocked into stillness.
The sudden noise of a passing truck seemed to snap
her back to reality. Deeply distressed, she fell on to
the couch and wept. Her tears were tears of anger;
anger at herself for hurting her friend, at Silvana for
actually loving one of their cruel, vicious enemies,
and anger at her family for drumming into her the
stories of rape, murder, and carnage. Mixed with her
anger was a sense of outrage. How could God allow
such things to happen?

'Silvana, you must hate me. I was terrible earlier on.'
Melina was standing in the doorway of Silvana's
house, her face pale and tear-streaked. She walked
through the door, putting both her arms around her
friend, started to say that she was sorry, but burst
into tears instead. For some moments, the two friends
stood in the doorway weeping and clinging to each
other.

'Come and sit down.' Silvana caught hold of herself

and, holding on to her friend's hand, guided her across the room and seated her close to herself.

The room felt cold, almost unlived-in; an atmosphere of heaviness hung over them.

Melina spoke quietly. 'I'm sorry I acted so hatefully; it was such a shock.'

'No, please don't apologise. I'm sorry for springing it on you so suddenly.'

For a moment the two friends sat, held hands and just looked at each other. In the background somewhere behind the house a woman was shouting to her son to come in. A large clock in the corner was ticking loudly and seemed to intensify the feeling of the moment.

'I've thought about what you said all afternoon. I can't understand how you could do it, but I'm your friend and I want to support you.' Again the friends hugged and now Silvana was weeping uncontrollably.

'I love him and he loves me. Why can't we marry, Melina?'

'I suppose you could,' said Melina,' but just think of what it would mean; think of both your families.'

Melina reached out with one hand and gently touched her friend's cheek. She wiped a tear away with her hand. 'Why don't you at least talk to the priest? He would be understanding.'

3

Father Dimitri

The city seemed to bustle with activity, but as Silvana turned down the path to the cathedral, she felt the atmosphere of peace and security that seemed to radiate from the old building. She had always loved this place, with its beautiful spires reaching joyfully towards the sky, and its neat gardens filled with the song of many birds all seeming to be singing praises to God. She looked about her, enjoying the air of seclusion. Then, taking a deep breath, she began to relax. A beautiful black butterfly with bright orange markings landed on her shoulder. She smiled. Surely everything would be all right. Peace and beauty were important to Father Dimitri, she knew, for he was always speaking about them as being essential to life. He would see the beauty of her love for Ali and help to bring about peace between their families.

The priest's attendant seemed reluctant to disturb him, but at last agreed to tell him of Silvana's request.

From outside the priest's study she heard the attendant ask hesitantly, 'Father Dimitri, there is someone to see you. Can she come in now?'

'Has she come for confession?' The old priest was immersed in his favourite past-time of transforming matchsticks into various objects of art. All around his little study were things he had created: matchstick cars, horses and carts and, his glory of glories, the matchstick cathedral that had taken two years to build. Upon its completion, it had been featured in a local newspaper and now was the object of admiration of all who came into his study.

'I'm not sure why she is here. She said it was not for confession but for personal advice.'

Father Dimitri looked at his watch, carefully placed some glue on the matchstick in his hand and then put it into place, absently nodding approval for the attendant to bring Silvana in.

Silvana walked into the room and kissed the priest's hand.

'Sit down here,' he said, placing her in the position where she could best admire his matchstick cathedral. 'What do you want?'

'I need help, Father.' Silvana felt as if she was going to cry but, swallowing, restrained herself. She looked pleadingly at her pastor. 'Father, I am in trouble.'

'Is this confessional? Because I really can't take time now; I'm very busy.' He looked across to the matchsticks and the little pot of glue.

'Father, I don't know if it is wrong or not, but I am in love.'

'You want me to marry you and your fiancé?' He

looked around at the clock.

'No, Father, please listen, I am in love with a Muslim.'

The atmosphere, which up to this point had been unsettled by the priest's evasiveness and evident longing to return to his hobby, suddenly became electric.

'You are what?! I missed that, I didn't hear properly.' He laughed nervously. 'I thought I heard you say you were in love with a Muslim.'

'It's true,' said Silvana, more confidently now that the words were out.

'My daughter!' The matchsticks forgotten, Father Dimitri stood up, drawing himself up to his full height, and spoke self-righteously. 'Do you know what that means? You would be joining yourself to the devil himself. All Muslims are possessed by Satan, they breathe evil with every breath, they are the apostate, they are the last curse of hell to come upon the earth!'

Silvana stood up, embarrassed, apologised as well as she could for disturbing him, and began to move towards the door. Why had she ever imagined he would understand? It was hopeless.

As her hand touched the doorknob, the priest pointed at her and shouted, 'You will be cast out of the church if you go through with this.' Then, in a calmer voice, but still roughly, he said, 'Why don't you join the women's choir? That will take your mind off such things.'

'Thank you, Father.' Silvana left the room politely, hurried past the attendant and stumbled down the stone stairs. By the time she had reached the bottom, she was crying. 'Oh God, can't you help me?' she sobbed.

The bus was crowded but Ali didn't seem to mind. The loud music thumping out from the radio beside the driver was numbing. Those passengers trying to communicate with each other were shouting, yet, even then, it seemed they had to lip-read to understand each other. The clouds of cigarette smoke hung heavy in the air and the atmosphere was, if anything, quite depressing. Yet, in the midst of this, Ali was excited; for he had decided to visit Silvana at her home and ask her to marry him, not caring what anyone thought.

Looking out of the window as the bus sped along, he could see life being acted out before him; crowds of people, some rich, some poor, some going to mosque, some going to church. Yet basically he knew that they were the same at heart, with the same basic needs.

As the bus turned the last corner before reaching Silvana's town, Ali felt a surge of apprehension. How would he get to see her? He could hardly walk up to her door and ask her father if she was at home.

The bus stopped and Ali sat still as all the other passengers filed out. For a moment he felt that perhaps he should just stay on the bus and return home. Perhaps everyone was right, perhaps there was no hope, the system could not be beaten. Almost unconsciously, Ali found himself walking down the aisle of the bus and out on to the crowded street, with the noise of horns honking and people shouting.

Maybe just to walk near her house would be sufficient. To be near her was all he really wanted. As Ali walked along, he saw a park, and almost unconsciously found himself going into it, glad to leave the hectic hubbub of the street.

There was a path that went directly through the park with trees on either side, curving in its ascent as slowly, and then rapidly, it became a steep hill. After a while he reached the crest. Below him was a view over the whole town.

'Silvana, I know you are there somewhere; I so long to be with you,' Ali whispered. Over to the left he could see the cathedral standing proudly above the surrounding buildings. Just a block or two away, or so it seemed, was a large mosque.

The sun was gradually sinking, and the cathedral and mosque began slowly to become mere outlines against the evening sky. Ali watched and wondered if it would ever be possible for the mosque and cathedral to be brought together. Both were buildings dedicated to God, although of different shapes and traditions; and both were filled with people somehow trying to reach out to a God who seemed totally beyond them. Each was convinced that their way of reaching God was right, and that the others were wrong.

For a moment, Ali seemed to have an inner sense that perhaps both groups could be wrong. 'Wouldn't it be wonderful,' he thought to himself, 'if God could reach down to people instead of people having to reach up to Him. Then it wouldn't matter what the shape of the building was, or history, or prejudice, or anything. God could reach down to man.' For a

moment Ali felt a surge of hope; but then as he
looked back to the solid black outlines of the mosque
and the cathedral, the abrupt disillusionment hit him.
It was easy to dream, but reality was something else.
There was no hope, no hope at all.

4

The Telephone Call

The next day Melina and Silvana were sitting in Silvana's house.

The warmth of the kerosene heaters and the cosy effect of the paintings neatly hung around the walls gave a friendly, secure, setting for their evening together; so different from the last time they had been there.

'I'm sorry that I ever went to that church. It was incredible. You know what they say about the matchsticks? Well, it's true. He has them everywhere.'

Melina laughed. She was glad that her friend seemed a little more relaxed, despite her embarrassing experience at the church.

Silvana stood up and began to walk around the room and to straighten some of the photographs in the frames.

'I can see now that the Christian faith is merely traditional, part of our cultural heritage. Let's be honest, Melina, we are moved by it in a sentimental way, but it doesn't really affect how we are as people; you know, deep inside us.'

Melina wasn't sure what Silvana was leading up to but she agreed, feeling the same way. It was a link with their own culture more than anything directly concerned with God.

'Mel,' Silvana spoke slowly. She hadn't called her friend Mel for years, since they were very young. 'What would you say if I became a Muslim?'

Melina rolled her eyes and reached out for the box of matches lying on the table. She pulled a couple of matches out, creased her face, and peered at the matches as if she were shortsighted. 'I think you had better join the choir, dear.'

Both the girls collapsed in peals of laughter.

After they had calmed down, Silvana looked up at the ceiling; 'I just love him so much! I think I would even be willing to change my religion to marry him.'

Melina took her friend's hand and looked very seriously and deeply into her eyes. 'Silvie,' – she too had resorted to their childhood pet names – 'when you told me the other day, I couldn't believe my own reaction. I was so angry and hostile. If I felt like that, how do you think your family will react? Especially if you start talking about changing your religion.'

'I know, I know! But I just feel trapped in the system, so totally stuck.'

In the distance the call to prayer could be heard coming from the mosque. Looking across to her friend, Melina said softly, 'Silvie, if there *is* a God, maybe He can help you.'

Not far away, Ali was sitting in the tea house and beginning to drink his third glass of tea. The idea of going back home without seeing Silvana was unthinkable, yet he had not yet worked out how he could see her.

Ali smiled as he looked across the tea house. It was crowded with men playing backgammon, a television blaring in one corner, a man with a flute playing in another corner and everyone shouting at the same time. He thought that it was a clear picture of the confusion and blindness of the world he lived in.

Suddenly an idea flashed into his mind. He would telephone Silvana's home and if her father or mother answered, he would just apologise for ringing the wrong number and hang up.

He trembled as he fumbled with the token to put in the telephone slot.

'Hello, Silvana, it's Ali,' he whispered, when she answered. 'Can you talk?'

'Yes, my parents are out. I'm here with my friend.'

'Silv, I just had to hear your voice; I can't stand not seeing you.'

For some moments the two talked and laughed with each other. Melina, watching from the far side of the room, saw the transformation as her friend, tired and pale, turned into a fresh, lively personality. She laughed, giggled and sighed, clasping the telephone to the side of her face as if it were Ali himself Melina looked on, wondering what on earth Ali was telling her to create such an effect.

'Can you meet me now?' he was asking.

'Oh, Ali, how can I? My parents would kill me if they found out. I know. I could leave a note to say

I'm staying at Melina's. After I've seen you, I can go to her house, so no one will know. I'll take a shawl and wait for you outside the post office. I'll have to hurry before it gets dark.'

Silvana hung up the phone and rushed across the room, screeching like a chicken. 'Oh Melina,' she gasped as she collapsed back onto the sofa, 'he's wonderful,' Melina looked on, smiled, and then turned serious.

'He is making you deceitful by doing this.'

Silvana stopped and looked at her friend, a little angry at her response. 'I know, but what else can I do? What would you do? Ring Father Dimitri and ask him to be a chaperon?'

Reluctant to spoil her friend's joy, Melina said no more. Silvana scurried around getting ready, looking for the shawl that would disguise her, and arranging to come to Melina's house later that evening. Then, the shawl in place, she hurried out of the house towards her rendezvous.

5

Together

Walking, hand in hand, up the same path Ali had earlier walked alone, was a wonderful experience for both of them.

The pain of separation was temporarily forgotten. Being together was all that mattered at this point.

Silvana's face glowed with joy; her hair was fresh and alive, and her innocent eyes disarmed Ali and made him feel that he could never be unkind to her.

As they neared the hill overlooking the city, Ali paused, looking thoughtful. Slowly he turned and smiled tenderly at Silvana. 'What I've done tonight is wrong, to make you deceive your parents, Silvie,' he said, not knowing that this had been her childhood name. 'I promise you that I have no intentions to make you do anything that makes you feel guilty.'

Silvana looked at Ali and loved him even more than she had before. By now they were overlooking the town, the sun had completely disappeared and the cathedral and the mosque were again just silhouettes against the sky.

'Also, Silvie, I've decided that I'm willing to change my religion and become a Christian so that we can marry.'

Silvana burst into laughter. Ali, taken aback by her response, was shocked and looked a little offended.

'Oh Ali, I'm sorry. It's just that this afternoon I decided I would be willing to become a Muslim to marry you.'

Together they laughed and both turned and looked out across the city. There was an intense look of sorrow in Ali's eyes. The wavy line of hair at the front of his face that never would lie down properly exaggerated his look of helplessness.

'Silvie, I love you deeply; in fact, I can't even begin to tell you the way that I feel about you. It's like I don't know where I end and you begin. It's like, well, like we are one.' Reaching out with his right hand he stroked the side of her face.

Silvana's large brown deer-like eyes began to fill with tears. 'Oh Ali, why does it have to be this way?' Slumping forward she buried her face in his chest.

For a moment that seemed eternal, Ali's warm arms enfolded her protectively. At first the thought of saying, 'It's all right' came to his mind, then the realisation that it wasn't all right flooded his soul.

'Silvie, I'm lost without you, I love you.' The words stumbled from his lips. Abruptly, he moved away and kicked moodily at a tree. Looking up to heaven, he silently pleaded for help; 'God? You're there, we know that. But how can we know the truth? Why can't our love overcome the differences?'

As he looked around at Silvana, he was more aware than ever before of the distance between their different cultures.

'I can't make you leave your family, your religion, and your friends, I just can't do it. Oh – as much as I long to be with you I can't force you into a lifetime of isolation from everything that is familiar to you.'

'But Ali, I want to be with you! I'm willing to leave it all behind just to be with you.' Silvana stretched out her hands imploringly. 'Ali, why can't we break the system? Why can't we show that love can overcome all those areas of pain and hate that divide our people?'

The evening, which earlier had been warm, had now turned cool. There was a clearness in the atmosphere and the sky had burst forth into a display of sparkling stars that illuminated their path.

'Come, I want to show you something.' Ali led the way, holding Silvana's hand, to where he had stood the night before.

Standing and looking over the city was usually an exhilarating experience and should have been an intensely romantic setting, but tonight their feelings were overshadowed by a sense of despair.

'Look down there, darling.' Ali pointed with his other hand. 'A cathedral and a mosque, and look, both buildings have their lights on and people are inside. Both are convinced they are right and the other group is wrong.' Ali turned and looked deeply into Silvana's eyes. 'Both sets of people are reaching up to God in some religious way, yet I'm sure they are both missing God.' He let go her hand, walked a pace away, and then turned. 'Silvie, just think of this. If God reached down to man, instead of man reaching up to God, then it wouldn't matter what religion or what culture or what country we came from. But, but...!' He looked down at the ground and became even more sombre; 'He hasn't reached down to us. That's why it's all so hopeless.'

The air felt even colder as the two stood there, as if rooted to the ground for one intense moment. They were lost in a system that was beyond their control; not of their making, or choosing, yet neither was it within their ability to break it down.

Ali led Silvana to a bench and as they sat down, she thought how much she loved him. His face, although drawn by losing a whole night's sleep, had such an open and sensitive expression. Slowly turning towards her, he smiled; not his usual full smile but a painful, almost weak, attempt at comfort.

'Silvie,' – Ali's eyes dropped to the ground as he hesitated for one long moment – 'I can't go through with it. I can't force you into a life away from your family. And yet... yet I can't even imagine what life lived without you would be like.'

Silvana's large brown eyes gazed into his, as if delving deeply into her beloved's soul.

'Silvie, if you come away with me, it means we will have each other and no one else. We will be rejected by both our families and even by most of our friends.'

In the distance a strange sound seemed to echo their pain. Church bells began to ring just as the evening call to prayer was being made. It was a weird sensation of religious confusion that seemed to epitomise their own dreadful dilemma. Through the noise, Silvana spoke softly.

'Ali, to be with you is the most important thing in my life. I cannot even begin to consider being apart from you.'

Ali got up abruptly from the seat and turned to face her.

'My precious, precious love,' he said, taking both her hands in his, 'I will go to the post office tomorrow. If you decide to come with me, we will run away from it all and be married. We will leave the religions of our fathers and the prejudices of history and start a fresh new life together.'

'Oh Ali, I will come, I will, I will!' Ali reached out gently and put one finger upon her lips, quietening her spontaneous response.

'But if you are not there by one o'clock tomorrow, I will know that you realised the cost of our love was too great to leave behind everything that has been your life until now.'

Silvana kissed his finger and then smiled. 'Ali, I love you and I will be there.' For one moment they held each other tightly. The church bells had stopped ringing; the call to prayer was a mere echo. The night was cool and yet electric with expectancy.

6

The Letter

The sun tumbled into Silvana's room, bringing warmth and the expectancy of a new start. She stirred. A smile crossed her face, her eyelids fluttered open. She stretched, and then bounced out of bed. A little tune began to sing in her heart, and she ran to the windows and looked out. 'Ah –,' she said, in a long drawn-out breath, 'it's going to be a lovely day!'

With mounting excitement she bathed, taking extra care in the choice of her dress and the arrangement of her hair. Today she would see her beloved and she must look her best.

Once dressed, she went through her belongings carefully, selecting a few things she could carry easily in a little overnight bag.

In the kitchen, as she helped her mother prepare breakfast, a little smile kept quivering around her lips.

'You look happy this morning,' commented her mother. 'Did you have a nice time with Melina?'

'Oh yes, it was lovely. Here, let me pour you some coffee.'

'Thanks, my dear. Why don't you ask your father to come and eat his breakfast while it's hot?'

Later, after breakfast, Silvana slipped up to her room. She must leave a note for her parents so that they would not worry. Sitting down at her desk, she took a pen and began to write:

Dearest Mummy & Daddy,

I love you both very much. I appreciate all you have given me and all you have taught me. But now I must make a choice which has not been easy for me. It is not meant to hurt you.

I am in love with a young man who is a Muslim. We are going to be married. He is good and honest and I know you would like him if you only gave yourself a chance to get to know him.

I hope you will forgive me and that we can still be as close as we've always been.

I love you,

Silvana

As she signed her name she frowned. How she hoped her parents would understand her decision and still love her! She wanted to please them, and yet she realised that the letter was bound to upset them. She sighed, folded the letter and propped it up on her desk. Looking at her watch, she realised that she had some spare time. Suddenly, she thought of leaving some flowers for her mother with the letter. A parting gift might offset the pain of her news and her departure. Without another thought, she left the letter on her desk and hurried out of the house and down the street to the local flower seller.

While she was away, her mother came into the room looking for her, and instead found the letter on the desk. Puzzled, she began to read it. Then, the colour ebbing from her face, she began to scream hoarsely, and collapsed weeping on to the floor.

Silvana's father, Petros Silvanou, heard the noise and came rushing into the room.

'What's the matter? Are you all right?'

'It's Silvana. My poor baby she is lost to us forever.' Trembling hands held out the letter.

Nervously, Silvana's father took it and began to read. 'A Muslim! A dirty, filthy Muslim! I'll kill him! He will never touch my daughter.'

'It's too late,' her mother sobbed, 'it's too late. We have lost her.'

Angrily, Petros crumpled the letter in his fist. Then, in despair, his hand fell to his side and the letter fell to the floor.

That morning, as Ali stood outside the post office, he was remembering the cobbled street in his home town that he had played on as a child. He would walk along making sure he didn't step on any of the cobblestones that had cracks in them. In his young mind, he had imagined that just to stand on a cracked cobblestone would bring him bad luck. Today Ali's left foot stood on such a stone. Yet his adult mind rejected the superstitions of the past. His future with Silvana, their day-to-day life together, would prove that superstition was worthless, and their marriage itself would be a demonstration of how true love could overcome all prejudice and historical antagonisms.

He looked once again at his watch; in fact, his attention was divided between his watch and looking up the street towards where Silvana would appear. In a short while his beloved would be here and they would depart and begin a life of beauty together. The street was crowded. People seemed to be rushing, shouting and haggling all around him, totally unaware of the importance of the moment.

Near him was a tree that stood alone amidst all the hubbub of city life. The leaves seemed tired, coated with the pollution of the city. Yet the natural green life shone through, like an oasis in the midst of all the petrol fumes and noise, giving Ali fresh hope. The thought that Silvana might not come never entered his mind. He was confident that her intense love and devotion to him would bring her to his side.

Meanwhile, Silvana still stood with her back to the wall, the flowers clutched close, weeping and pleading with her father – 'Let me go, let me go!'

'Let you go, for what? To tie your body and soul to a Muslim? I would rather kill you first!'

'Oh Papa, please, let me go, I love him. I can't live without him!' The pain in her face and voice was almost unbearable.

The little room, which had previously been a place of joy and expectancy, was now filled with an atmosphere of gloom and foreboding.

'You don't understand, Papa, we love each other. Oh please, please let me go!' Silvana dropped to her knees, the flowers scattered about her, and grasped her father's legs. In one swift move he cast her off and she tumbled to the ground. Her mother sat speechless in a chair in the corner, moaning and rocking herself backwards and forwards.

Her father bent down and with one hand grabbed Silvana by her long black hair and jerked it back viciously. Through the tears, she looked pleadingly up towards this man who was her father, her own flesh and blood, the one who had given her life.

She could see his hand descending like a mighty weapon but did not try to resist. The pain at the instant his hand smashed into her face was intense. She tasted the blood on her lip and felt it trickle down the side of her mouth. Yet the pain of her broken heart far outweighed her physical suffering.

She lay still and sobbed, as the shouting went on and on. It seemed an age later when the abuse, cursing and occasional blows finally ceased. Petros stood, his back still rigid with emotion and anger, looking out of the window into the street. Her mother sat in the chair, silently rocking to and fro with a look of helplessness.

Suddenly, a burst of energy shot through Silvana's soul. She raised herself up and looked at the clock. Four o'clock. It was too late. She had been shouted at and cursed for over five hours. In agony she sank again to the ground. Ali was gone, he would think she did not truly love him. The sense of pain was so great she thought she would die.

Ali had refused to give up hope, and yet walked about with rising anxiety. About four o'clock he gave up. As he boarded the bus for his home he looked around one last time towards the post office. His heart ached and he felt the burden of life was too great to bear. As the bus drew out of the city, he pressed his forehead against the window. The vibration blurred his vision. 'Goodbye, Silvana,' he whispered, a tear slowly beginning to trickle down his cheek. 'Goodbye for ever . . . for ever.' He closed his eyes, leaned forward in the seat, buried his face in his hands and wept unashamedly.

7
Mavramati

Silvana moaned, tossed restlessly, and then opened her eyes. The light in the centre of the ceiling seemed to be spinning around, and she had the sensation of falling down a long tunnel. Slowly her eyes focused on a flower on the wallpaper. The sound of a fly buzzing nearby brought her back to reality, and she jerked upright in the bed. 'No! Oh no!' Her hands nervously clasped and crumpled the bed covers. 'No!' The cry seemed torn from the depths of her being. 'I failed, oh, what shall I do?' Throwing herself on her pillow she sobbed in despair.

The door quietly opened and closed. 'Silvie? It's me. Are you all right?' Melina gently laid her hand on her shoulder.

'What shall I do?' sobbed Silvana.'Oh, whatever shall I do? I just want to die.'

'Silvie, your face! It's so bruised. Whatever has happened? And why are you so upset?'

Silvana explained brokenly, still shaken by sobs. 'They found out I was going to marry Ali. Father beat me and wouldn't let me go. Now it's too late. It's too late, and I want to die.'

Melina took Silvana's hand and gently held it. 'Surely there must be another answer besides death. Ali would be hurt to see you like this.'

'No, by now he must hate me. He trusted me. I was to meet him by one o'clock and if I didn't come he would know I didn't truly love him. He will think I was insincere. Oh, what shall I do?' Fresh sobs wracked her body. 'I love him and he will never know.'

'But Silvie, surely you could write to him or something and tell him what happened.'

'I don't know where he lives! There is no hope. Oh, Mel, help me. Please help me.'

Melina embraced her friend, holding her tightly and rocking back and forth as though she were comforting a small child. 'It will be all right. Really it will. Somehow God will work things out for you. You'll see.'

Just two days later Melina thought of these words as she sat beside Silvana's bedside in the stark, sterile atmosphere of a hospital room. A bird, singing outside the window, seemed to bring a message of hope to her shocked mind. As if in response, Silvana started to stir and moan. Melina took hold of her hand, and was ready when her friend's brown eyes flickered open.

'Where am I? How did I get here?'

'You're in hospital, Silvie. They brought you in for a stomach pump about three hours ago. Your father found you on the floor in your room. You nearly died, Silvie. The doctor said they only just got you in time.'

Silvana looked at her friend through her tears. 'Oh Mel, you are the only one I've got now.' A nurse walked into the room and looked sternly at both girls; yet, as she saw the pain that was so evident in Silvana's eyes, for one moment her harshness softened.

'Let me carry it for you.' Melina took Silvana's case as they walked down the steps from the hospital a few days later.

'Oh, Mel, I feel so shaky!'

'Do you want a taxi?'

'No, the walk will probably clear my head. I need it to be clear when I see Mother and Father.'

'Have you decided what to say to them?'

'No – I expect things will carry on somehow.'

Silvana stopped for a brief moment and looked seriously at her friend. 'Tell me, Mel, do you think there is a God?'

Melina was surprised at the change of subject.

'Yes, of course I do.'

'Do you understand Him? I mean, do you think He is personal, someone who cares?'

Melina looked at her friend and couldn't help thinking how much Silvana had aged in the last week. She was really acting in a very strange way. 'I don't know, Silv, I really don't know.'

The two girls walked on in silence.

'Aysha, I've got to talk to you!'

Ali's desperation had driven him at last to his cousin's front door. He thought once again what a very beautiful young woman Aysha was. She had an innocent, open face framed by lovely black hair which fell in curls to her shoulders. At this moment her large brown eyes were sympathetic and concerned.

'Of course, Ali, do come in.'

Aysha's home, like herself, seemed to radiate warmth and serenity. Ali began to relax as he poured out his troubles.

'Aysha, I'm sick, really sick. I've fallen in love with a Christian girl. We were going to run away together but she couldn't go through with it.' Ali looked down at the carpet with its interwoven pattern. He felt his voice crack as if he was going to cry, but contained himself.

'Aysha, I feel so bad, so sick with pain, I want to die.'

Aysha's eyes showed great concern. She nodded and let Ali continue.

'Well, I just can't get it out of my mind. I can't eat, I can't sleep, I can't study. I feel like I'm alive and yet dead inside; like the most precious thing in my life has been smashed in pieces before my eyes.'

Aysha nodded again in an understanding way, sat back and looked lovingly at her cousin. 'Ali, love is something that is so complicated.' She looked down for a moment and then went on, 'You remember the story about the Taj Mahal?'

Ali nodded. Aysha's warm personality seemed to generate comfort. He felt better just being with her.

'Well, the Taj Mahal, that palace in India that is

considered the most beautiful building in the whole world, was built by a prince. He built it to retain the memory of his love for his beloved wife. They were separated by her death, yet the memory of her life and love was so precious to him that he expressed it by building a beautiful palace. I think what you need to do is build a Taj Mahal for this Christian girl you love.'

'What do you mean?' Ali smiled at Aysha's philosophical way of putting things.

Aysha leaned across and touched his hand gently. 'There is a compartment of your heart that you can keep for her. You should build a monument in your heart for this girl. Allow the sorrow that you are feeling now to be the foundation stone. Then determine that every time you have to make a decision, to do that which is good and right; do it in memory of your love for her.'

'Aysha! Where on earth did you think all this up? I didn't realise you were so deep.'

Aysha smiled sadly, then fixed her eyes upon the carpet as Ali had done a few moments earlier. When she looked up, Ali could see that her eyes were swollen with tears, and her own inner pain was evident. She said softly, 'I'm building a monument to a memory also.' She looked away, bit her lip and then suddenly smiled and quickly wiped her eyes.

'But that's a different story,' she continued briskly. She looked at Ali closely. 'We need to use our pain constructively; we musn't let the overwhelming sense of loss destroy us.'

For a brief moment Ali looked at this young woman, his own cousin, and felt that she had wisdom beyond anything he had ever encountered. 'Thank you, Aysha, thank you so much.'

'Do you realise how old he is?' Silvana's mother looked sternly at her husband.

'It was your brother's idea! He said if we married her off, it would solve the problem.' Petros Silvanou looked away.

'But he is fifty-three years old – he is our age. Can you imagine what it will be like for her to marry him?'

Silvana's father turned towards his wife again. 'But what else can we do? Of course, this would not have been our first choice, but in the circumstances, the very fact he is willing to have her is good. Everyone is talking about it; we have been utterly shamed by the whole thing. He has even agreed not to force her to go for the tests at the doctor's. Who knows what those two got up to!'

An atmosphere of doom hung over the room, as the couple stood alone in their sorrow, with no one to turn to for help. Petros spoke at last, heavily.

'Call her in and we will tell her what we have planned.'

Silvana stood motionless by the window. Her face, stained with tears, was expressionless and her eyes, portraying hope that had died, stared vacantly into space.

In the far-away regions of her mind she heard a bell ringing; voices, then footsteps on the stairs. Melina came into the room.

'Silvie, are you all right? Can you hear me? I knocked on the door but you didn't answer.'

Woodenly Silvana turned, walked over to the bed and sat down.

'What has happened?' Melina nervously raised her voice. 'Silvie, speak to me.'

'I'm to be married, sold to the highest bidder,' said Silvana flatly.

'Married! To whom?'

'Stavros Mavramati.' The words were spat out with disgust, horror and disbelief.

'Oh no! Not him! You must be mistaken.'

Silvana sneered. 'My dear parents are trying to save me from the deathly clutches of a Muslim.'

'Oh Silv, I'm sure they aren't trying to hurt you.'

'Mel, I can't marry him. How can they even think of such a sick idea? I would rather be dead than even let him touch my hand. He is evil. Oh, why does there have to be so much pain? So much unkindness?'

Melina took hold of her friend's hand. 'Oh Silv, it's so unbelievably complicated, it's like one of those wretched tear-jerking movies. You can't go through with it, that's for sure, but what is the answer?'

Melina poured a glass of tea from the tray on the bedside table, sat back on the bed and looked closely at her friend. Silvana's eyes were dull and full of pain, like those of a wounded deer. 'How did you react when they told you?'

'It's strange, but I didn't believe it. I actually laughed. Father looked so confused. I suggested if he liked I could marry Father Dimitri as well. Mother was shocked, as though I had blasphemed or something. I thought Father was going to hit me, but he just told me it was arranged and there was nothing I could do about it.'

Melina leaned forward and put her empty glass on the table. 'How did you react then?'

Silvana looked down as if ashamed. 'I said I would keep trying to kill myself until I succeeded. Mel, it's terrible. I just can't face living without Ali.' Her eyes began to fill with tears. 'And the thought of being married to Stavros Mavramati is worse than death itself.'

Stavros Mavramati was sitting with his feet on the desk when the mail arrived. Quickly leafing through the bills and notices, he noticed a handwritten envelope. Opening it, he read:

> Dear Mr Mavramati,
>
> We appreciate your interest in our daughter and are very flattered that you wish to marry her. However, we feel that, at the moment, Silvana is not ready for marriage.
>
>   Sincerely,
>
>   *Petros Silvanou*

The noise of Mavramati's fist crashing down on the desk was followed by a string of profanities.

'Androula!'

'Yes sir.' His secretary sidled nervously into the room. 'Did you call me?'

'You know I called you. Where does Petros Silvanou work?'

'At the Success Catering Company.'

A sneering smile crossed Mavramati's face. 'Good. Get the file on Father Dimitri Georgeou.'

The secretary walked across the room to the filing cabinet.

'Ah, Mavramati, Mavramati, come in.'

'Father Dimitri! It's nice to see the roof repaired and looking in order.'

Father Dimitri beckoned his visitor to sit down. The setting was predictable; matchsticks lying everywhere around his desk. The Holy Bible, covered with dust, was acting as a board on which matchsticks were being carefully glued together.

'What can I do for you, Mavramati?'

Stavros Mavramati looked piercingly across the desk. He was a man of intense personality, and great wealth and power. 'Two questions really, Father. Firstly, what is the church's attitude to my marrying Silvana Silvanou, considering that I have already been divorced twice? Before you answer, let me remind you where the money for your new roof came from.'

Father Dimitri looked away nervously. His matchstick cathedral was a symbol of his creativity, and yet was also a graphic illustration of his weakness and lack of contact with the real world.

'No problem, Mavramati, no problem. We can arrange things so that there is no awkwardness. What is your second question?'

Stavros Mavramati looked closely at his spiritual adviser and moved forward slightly. He reached down into his brief-case. 'I have a legal document here for you to sign to sell me your share in the property and business of the Success Catering Company.'

'Sell? It's out of the question. You must be . . .' Mavramati raised his hand imperiously for silence.

'Please look at these photographs and then reconsider.'

Father Dimitri's fingers trembled as he fumbled with the envelope. He looked down, gasped and closed his eyes. Sweat beads built up like great globules on his forehead. 'How did you . . .?'

'Never mind,' Mavramati sneered. 'Just sign here.' The contract slid across the desk top, ploughing a furrow between the loose matchsticks.

Stavros Mavramati's yellow teeth leered as the priest signed the document. He reached out his hand, snatched the document, and waved it in the air. 'I intend to get this girl. I want her to amuse me and nothing is going to stand in my way.' He stood and looked down at the broken form of the older man. 'By the way, I will be making a large contribution to your church. I would like new seats ready there for the wedding.'

8

Costas

Costas was a typical Greek youth, who felt he could conquer the world. He was strong and rugged with wavy black hair, which framed a face that was not handsome and yet had an attraction that made people look at him twice. Perhaps it was the friendly twinkle in his almost black eyes that was so appealing.

He had just recently returned from university and on an impulse decided to pay a visit to his father's uncle and aunt. He hadn't seen his cousin Melina in two years and now, when she walked into the room, he was taken aback. Melina the tomboy was now a poised young woman.

'Costas, what a surprise!'

'Hello, Melina. It seems you have grown up. Don't tell me you no longer climb trees,' he said, with mock seriousness.

'Costas! No, I don't climb trees any more. I've grown respectable.'

'Respectable? You? I don't believe it.'

As they laughed, Melina's father entered the room. He was a jovial man, middle-aged, portly and nearly bald.

'What are you two up to? Ah, Costas, it is good to see you.'

The two men kissed each other on each cheek.

Melina's mother came in with a tray of goodies and cups of steaming tea. 'Costas, you look hungry. Don't they feed you at that college?'

'Auntie,' Costas laughed, 'you will never change. You're always trying to fatten me up.' They hugged, then Melina's mother began to bustle around, trying to coax everyone to eat.

They spent a pleasant hour together before Costas said his goodbyes.

As he walked down the lane, he thought about Melina. She was an attractive girl and not flighty like some of the girls at university. She would make someone a good wife. He smiled to himself, thinking he must be getting old to be thinking about marriage.

'Mel, come quickly. Oh Mel, you'll never guess! I'm so happy, I can't believe it.'

'Calm down, calm down.' Melina took Silvana's hand and led her to the sofa.

'Well, Mother has somehow convinced Father that it would be wrong to force me to marry Stavros Mavramati.' She leaned back, looked upwards and sighed. 'He's called the wedding off!'

'Oh, Silvie!' Melina squeezed her friend's hand and then reached across and hugged her. 'That's wonderful news.'

Silvana sat up and smiled. 'Mel, I feel for the first time that maybe there is hope. Somehow, in spite of all this, maybe Ali and I can be drawn together.'

'You know, Silv, I have been doing a lot of thinking. You know what you asked me once about God? Maybe there really is a God who is interested in us and who wants to be involved in our lives.'

Silvana focused her eyes on the bowl of fruit on the table. 'Perhaps; but to change the subject, who was that you were talking to in church on Sunday?'

A faint tinge of colour spread over Melina's face. 'Oh, my father is his father's uncle.'

'Mel, why are you blushing?'

'I'm not blushing, it's just hot in here.'

'What's his name?' Silvana grinned.

'Costas. But why are you looking like that? He's just a relative.'

The sun poured through the window into Silvana's bedroom. She felt warm inside, as a deep sense of relief spread over her that she did not have to marry Stavros Mavramati. The clock on the table said half-past eight. She stretched, and then decided to bask in the enjoyment of the moment before getting up. Thoughts of Ali broke into the peacefulness, bringing feelings of frustration that he still didn't know that she had tried to come to meet him. But just as a wonderful dream of what could have been filled her mind, she was shaken back to reality by her mother coming into the room. 'Quick,' her mother panted, out of breath, her hand fluttering nervously to her chest, 'you must get dressed quickly.'

Startled, Silvana sat up. 'Why? Is something wrong?'

'It's Stavros Mavramati. He is downstairs talking to your father.'

'Oh, but Mother, we agreed I didn't have to marry him. Why do I even have to see him?'

Her mother looked into her beloved daughter's eyes, and then away. 'It is best to be prepared if anything goes wrong,' she said evasively.

Downstairs, Silvana's father was speaking. 'We have considered the situation more thoroughly, Mr Mavramati, and we have decided that we are not going to give Silvana to you in marriage.'

Stavros Mavramati looked up sharply. For a moment a frown creased his forehead, then an evil smile crossed his lips. 'Who do you work for these days?'

'For the Success Catering Company; why do you ask?'

'Do they own this house?'

'Yes, they do own the house, but I can't see how that is any concern of yours.'

Mavramati turned slowly with his back towards his host, plucked a flower out of the vase, crushed it, then turned, and said in a sinister voice, 'You are wrong both times. You see, I recently acquired both the catering company and this house. The simple truth is, you work for me and you live on my property.'

A wave of nausea swept over Silvana's father. 'But surely you wouldn't use that to force me to give you my daughter? Why, I could never get another job or house like this at my age.'

Stavros Mavramati drew close to him. His clammy, bumpy skin intensified the picture of a large, ugly toad. 'Let us put it this way. I want to marry your daughter very much; very much indeed. I do not intend that anything should stand in my way.'

The door opened and Silvana came into the room accompanied by her mother. Her normally outgoing personality was subdued, and she stood pale and quiet. Her large brown eyes widened in fear as she saw the look on her father's face.

Gazing across at Silvana, Mavramati's eyes wandered over her body, with a possessive look of greed and lust. 'I will come back tomorrow for your answer.' The words sounded sinister. With a nod to Silvana's mother, he turned and left the room.

For an instant Silvana closed her eyes, squeezing them tightly shut, almost as if to blot out the last sight of Mavramati.

'Answer? What did he mean, Daddy? You already told him the answer was no, didn't you? Daddy, tell me what happened!' Her voice rose with hysteria.

'I'm sorry, Silvana, I did my best.' Her father looked defeated; it seemed that he had suddenly aged ten years.

Fear clutched her heart and her words came out brokenly. 'Best? Best? What – what do you mean? Why are you sorry?'

Hesitantly, her father told them of his conversation with Mavramati.

Silvana stood paralysed, then, shaking her head as though to physically rid herself of such thoughts, she angrily stamped her foot. 'No, Daddy. You can't do this to me. It isn't fair!'

Petros stood as if rooted to the ground for a brief moment. He looked nervously at his wife and then pleadingly at his only daughter. 'What am I to do? It means my job and our home if we refuse him.' Holding out his hand to Silvana he continued uncertainly, 'It would be selfish of you to allow us to lose our home and security.'

'Selfish!' Silvana exploded. Turning to her mother she pleaded, 'Mamma, do something. I can't believe this is really happening to me. Please, please do something!'

9

Aysha

Aysha sat alone in the pretty garden outside her home. She loved this time of the year when the flowers seemed to be bursting with joy and colour. The birds sang joyfully in the trees and there was a freshness in the air which spoke of rebirth. Under normal circumstances, this was a time when most people were happy to be alive.

Despite the fact that the garden had a consoling influence upon Aysha's heart, she was, in fact, deeply burdened and deeply troubled. She had failed her family by forming a friendship with a young man at college.

Their relationship had been pure, and yet somehow deceit had crept into their experience. She had often deceived her parents about where she was going and who she was going to see. Still without telling her parents, she arrived at the conclusion that she was doing wrong and broke off the relationship. It had been painful for her and for her friend, but now the intensity of her love for him seemed to engulf and envelop her total being. Sitting alone in the garden, there was a strange numbing sense of emptiness that filled her heart. She so longed to be close to her friend, and yet at the same time knew that she had done the right thing.

She slowly bent over and smelled the sweet fragrance of an open rose; then she sighed, for the beauty of the flower itself seemed to have a certain kind of pain attached to it. Soon the fragrance would leave, the petals drop off and the stem would be bare. As she looked around the garden she was shaken by the bitter truth of nature that everything ultimately dies. Surely death transcended even the beauty she was presently experiencing! Looking towards the sky she whispered a prayer. She had no idea if God heard her or even if He cared. As she sat looking at the rose a little furry caterpillar slowly made its way up the stem, as if moving on a pilgrimage towards its destiny.

She reached out and tenderly stroked the soft furry form. Then, in one of those moments that is hard to explain, a sense of reasoning and understanding overwhelmed her. One day the little caterpillar would become a butterfly. She smiled as she lifted her eyes to the sturdy oak sheltering her from the sun. Why, death brings forth life! The end of one season is merely the ushering in of another. Without winter there is no spring, without spring there is no summer, and so the process would continue. Looking at the wondrous shapes of the clouds, she wondered how a God who could create such intense beauty, such order, such uniqueness all around her, could be so distant and difficult to know.

But then, she reasoned with herself, perhaps God is not so distant. Perhaps creation is a picture, a painting from the finger of a God who loves and is always present.

She stood up and walked down the garden path, looking out across the rolling hills. How she loved nature, and the country; how she loved the freshness and the purity that surrounded her! She thought of the old Sufi mystic poet whom she loved so dearly, whose words had bored their way into her soul when she first read them:

> 'If I could but see Your face O Lord,
> I would gladly die.'

A tear slid down her cheek as she spoke to a God who all her life she had believed was there, but whom she had, until now, believed could not be known in a personal, intimate way. 'O Lord,' she whispered, 'if I could but see Your face I would gladly die.' She uttered the words as a deep, heartfelt prayer. Assurance seemed to well up in her innermost being, that seemed to cry out in authoritative, comforting tones; 'You *will* see My face, My child.'

At this, the gentle heart of this sweet girl broke and she began to weep; deep, cleansing, purifying sobs that shook her body. Through her tears she said, 'O Allah, all I know of You is what I have been taught. Yet something inside of me says there is more, and that You are not distant and unconcerned. With the little knowledge that I have, I call You my Lord, whom I desire to know.'

Her eyes brightened at the awareness that she had begun a pilgrimage. She knew in her heart that it would not be a futile pilgrimage, but would be a journey in which she would discover the very meaning of life itself.

10

The Holy Book

The narrow winding pathway that led through the little wood down to the stream was a bower of fragrance, the sight of the flowers heralding all its intricate interweavings of colour and texture. Yet Silvana's heart was heavy as she walked with Melina.

'Melina, I feel like some evil fate is trying to destroy me. My world has come crashing around me just when I thought things were getting better. I am going to have to marry Stavros Mavramati after all.'

Melina paused, placing her hand on her friend's shoulder. 'What happened? I thought it was settled that the engagement was off.'

'For us, it was settled. My father told Mavramati and he became very angry. Evidently, he now owns the company Dad works for. If I don't marry Mavramati, he is going to fire Dad and kick us out of our home.'

'No!' Melina exploded. 'Why, that is blackmail. How can anyone be so evil and twisted to do such a thing? There must be something we can do. You can't just let him have his way.'

'Don't you think I have tried to think of a way around it? I would feel so guilty if I was to cause my parents to lose their home that I can't see any other way than to go through with it.'

Melina turned to her. 'Oh, Silvie, I feel so helpless. If only there was something I could do to help you.'

Silvana smiled and nodded slightly as if to communicate her gratitude. 'I feel like my life is ending. I keep thinking of Ali,' she faltered, and then burst into tears.

Quickly Melina put her arms around her and held her tightly.

'Oh Mel, I love him,' Silvana whispered between the sobs. 'I love him so much, I don't think I can bear it. Why is life so cruel?'

Melina had begun to cry as well. 'I don't know, Silv, I don't know.'

A squirrel darted up the side of the tree in front of them. Normally they would have giggled with delight, but today the burden of sorrow and hopelessness was so heavy that they were totally unaware of the beauty and promise of nature.

After talking to Costas, and sharing with him the thoughts she had been having about God, and her longing that God might be approachable, Melina felt more at peace.

The next day, Costas stopped at her house on his way to work to drop off a little package. Melina was upstairs, and so he left the parcel with her mother.

Her mother, hearing her daughter's footsteps on the stairs, called to her from the kitchen, 'Melina! Costas has just been here and he left this for you.'

'Oh.' Trembling, Melina tore the paper away, revealing a small black book with gold lettering. 'Look, Mamma.'

'The Holy Scriptures. Why ever did he give you that?'

'Because he knows I am interested in knowing about God.'

Her mother shook her head and turned back to making the bread. Melina ran up the stairs to her room and eagerly opened the book. 'Blessed are those who mourn, for they will be comforted.' What an idea, Melina thought.

'I've got to go back and see her, Aysha! I can't bear it any longer. I'm sure she really loves me.'

Aysha sat quietly. The little room in Ali's home lent itself to quietness. It was neat and clean, and yet gave the feeling of being lived in. A large handwoven rug hung on one wall, with several photos in frames on the other side. There was a picture of his great-grandmother who had died recently at the age of a hundred. He remembered sitting on her knee as a little boy; even then she had seemed ancient. 'Yoghurt and well water,' she used to tell him. 'Keep away from city water. Eat plenty of yoghurt and drink well water. That's what gives long life.'

Today the thought of long life was intolerable to Ali. It only meant he would have to carry the burden of his loneliness even longer. Aysha responded, 'I know it's terribly painful for you, but perhaps seeing her would only make things harder for her.'

Ali frowned. 'What do you mean?'

'Well, if she loves you, yet feels that she can't leave her family, her culture or religion behind, then she needs to have time on her own. That will allow her to overcome all the heartbreak that she must be experiencing. If you see her you may just add pain to her life.'

Ali dropped his head into his hands. 'That thought has crossed my mind. I think you are right.' He roughly rubbed his eyes as they began to swell with tears. 'But part of me is crying out just to be near her. I don't think I can stand it any longer.'

He gazed at the wall to avoid looking directly into Aysha's eyes. 'I have seriously considered killing myself. Every fibre in my being is yearning to be with her. I lie awake at night and just imagine seeing her beautiful eyes staring deeply into mine. I can't explain it, but when we were together, it was like feasting on something beautiful. It was as though something inside me was being fed with beauty and goodness. Sometimes, when I slip off to sleep, I dream that she is just a few yards away, but when I stretch out to her, I can never reach her hand.'

Aysha breathed out a long sigh. 'Oh Ali, you are tormenting yourself, and it hurts me to see you like this.'

Only the steady ticking of the clock broke the silence that had fallen on the room. Ali had laid his head on the crook of his arms, which were resting on the table. Suddenly he sat up, struck by a new idea.

'Aysha, will you go and see her?'

'Ali, I don't know if it will help either of you – it might make things more painful for her and for you.'

'Please, Aysha, I'm desperate!'

'Let me think about it and I'll let you know later today.'

Ali sat back and looked blankly up at the ceiling, then at the photographs neatly placed in their frames. He wondered if his great-grandmother was watching him from some other world. Another world! Increasingly the thought of a God who was distant and untouched by his problems came to his mind. If only there was a God in the universe who cared – cared about him and Silvana – cared about the pain he was suffering!

For a moment, his mind slipped back to the evening on the hill overlooking Silvana's city. He remembered the mosque and the cathedral, and remembered wishing God had reached down to man instead of leaving man to grope blindly, trying to reach up to God. The thoughts depressed him. Perhaps this distant God was laughing at him. If only, if only . . . Shaking his head as though trying to clear his mind, he looked back at the photographs and forced such thoughts out of his mind.

The candle in Costas's room slowly began to burn down. The shadows created by this unusual light reminded him of his childhood when power cuts were more common. Looking down into the pages of his new-found treasure, Costas felt as if his heart would burst at his new discovery. As he sat and pondered over the passages of this book with its enormous wisdom, he wondered how it was that he could have grown up in a church, and yet never personally read from the Holy Bible.

There was a scuffling sound outside the window. Probably cats, he thought absently to himself as he marvelled at the words he had just read. Jesus said, 'I no longer call you servants... Instead, I have called you friends.' The more he thought about it the more he wondered. God reaching down to man in Jesus Christ and setting up a new way whereby God and man could come into a relationship of friendship. This book showed God not as One who demands religious rituals, but as One who extends friendship and acceptance.

That afternoon on his way home, passing the frail elderly lady who sold flowers for her living, he had found himself stopping to chat with her and on impulse had bought a rose. Now he reached out to the flower in the vase. The soft, almost velvety look of the crimson rose was enhanced further by the candlelight. He smelt its sweetness and gently touched its petals. Surely the God who had created this had to be a God of goodness, friendship, beauty and love. The fragrance of the flower permeated the room. Sitting back in his chair, he began to think of Melina. She would be excited to hear of his discovery, a discovery that the Holy Scriptures talk of a God who cares, who reaches down to people walking the earth today and who says, 'I want you not as servants but as friends.'

The butterfly descended from the branch of the tree and fluttered past Melina and Costas as they stood in the garden behind Melina's house. The green of the trees seemed even richer after the gentle rain of the previous day.

'Costas, I'm terribly worried about Silvana,' Melina confided. 'It seems she is caught in a terrible trap. She loves a young man but is unable to marry him. Now, even worse, she is going to have to marry Stavros Mavramati. It's as if she has been caught in a spider's web.'

Costas nodded in an understanding way.

'I feel responsible for her as my friend, but totally helpless to know what to do.'

Melina's hazel eyes, which seemed to change colours, today seemed as green as a tree in spring. Costas noticed a tenderness about them he had not been aware of before.

Her face portrayed a great innocence that he was rapidly finding irresistible.

'You know, Melina, I really appreciate the way you care about Silvana.' Melina blushed and blinked her eyes in a girlish way. 'I feel that you are one of the kindest people I have ever met.'

Struggling to keep her composure, Melina said, 'It's kind of you to say that but what can I do to help her?'

'I think one of the most important things about friendship is just being there when you are needed, to listen, and to support.' Melina smiled and nodded, glad of the reassurance from one she was coming to respect more and more.

11

New Friends

Aysha knocked on the door and even at this late stage wondered if what she was doing was right. Silvana's mother opened the door slowly.

'Hello, may I see Silvana, please?'

'Yes, come in, she's upstairs. I will call her for you.'

Aysha looked about her. It was a nice home, yet she was aware of an odd, unhappy atmosphere, something she couldn't explain.

Silvana walked into the room and smiled hesitantly at her guest, whom she immediately found herself drawn to. Aysha was dressed in a modest way, wearing a pleated skirt and a grey sweater. Her long black hair hung loose, caught away from her face by a pale pink scarf, but it was her smile that attracted Silvana's attention. Somehow she felt that she would find understanding in this girl, no matter what she said to her.

'May I help you?'

'I hope so. I am the cousin of a very close friend of yours who asked me to visit you.'

'Please, do sit down. I will just make some tea and then we can chat.'

As Silvana left the room, Aysha found herself praying, 'Allah, she looks so unhappy. Help me to say something to draw her to Yourself.'

Silvana came back with a tray, which she placed on the table, and then handed her guest a cup of tea.

'Now, who is this mysterious friend who sent you?'

Aysha smiled tenderly. 'It is Ali.'

Silvana reeled back against the couch as though she had been hit. Her face turned white with fear.

'Silvana, are you all right?'

'What did he send you for? Does he hate me? I know. He is going to marry you, isn't he?'

'No, Silvana. He loves you and he lives in agony because he thinks you don't truly love him.'

'What? He still loves me? I was sure he would be angry with me because I didn't come. Then seeing you, as you are so beautiful, I thought surely he must love you. Does he really love me?'

'Yes, he does. He loves you very deeply.'

Tears began to stream down Silvana's face, and then, like a dam that had burst, all the pent-up emotions of the past few weeks found release as she began to sob. Aysha quickly moved to her side and put her arms around her. When the sobs had subsided, Aysha said gently, 'I'm afraid I don't understand. If you love Ali so much why didn't you meet him?'

'My parents found out and they stopped me. Father beat me and then locked me in my room.'

'Oh, Silvana, I'm so sorry.'

A bird flew to the windowsill and began to sing joyfully. Aysha spoke tenderly.

'God loves you. I'm sure if we trust Him, He will be able to work things out.'

'God?' Silvana laughed bitterly. 'What can He do? My father is being blackmailed into marrying me to Stavros Mavramati, an evil old man. There is no hope for me, not even from God.'

'Silvana, there is always hope when we throw ourselves on God's mercy. He loves you and He doesn't want you to be hurt.'

'Then why is He letting this happen to me?'

'Perhaps because the only way He can get your attention is through pain.'

Aysha's tone reached through Silvana's misery, and she looked up at her new friend.

'You sound as though that has happened to you.'

Aysha bowed her head, then looked up and smiled sadly. 'Yes, I refused to listen once and it was only when I lost the one I loved that I began to listen to God.'

The candle flickered, causing shadows to dance upon the wall in Ali's room. The centre of the flame seemed white and powerful. He sat and looked deeply into its glow.

His mind wandered back to the evening that he and Silvana had stood overlooking the city. The memory caused both pain and a kind of sweetness. But even more than the hurt he felt about Silvana was the intense sense of nothingness about just being alive. There seemed no real reason for birth, life, and death. It was just an involuntary happening, a sickening occurrence with no hope for anything beyond. He felt a chill run through his inner being, a cold sense of futility that had no reason or logic to it but was just there. Something strange and deep was bothering him in a way that he could not express in words. He looked at the clock. It was just after 3 a.m. He felt an inner tiredness, yet his mind was active. Perhaps that was the problem; if he could just numb his mind then the problems would no longer exist.

He thought of Aysha; her wisdom, and her strength of character. He thought of his mother, such a resigned woman, and his father, with his love for poetry and the old-style classical folk music. Then his thoughts returned to Silvana. Closing his eyes he tried to picture her face but found it blurry and hard to bring into focus. He thought of God. *A* God? *The* God? Gods? Who was right? Was there just one God? Did He care? Why was He so distant?

For a moment, his thoughts seemed to answer his questions. If God has created the earth in its beauty, surely He must be a God who is creatively sensitive, and given to fine detail.

Ali stood, walked across the room and looked out of the window. The moon was just a sliver, and yet projected a bright light. He turned and looked across at the candle. All right, so perhaps God was creative and sensitive, but why was He detached from people, distant, and isolated? He walked across to the candle and for a moment held his finger close to the flame. He moved it around, keeping just far enough away from the heat to avoid pain. Does God feel pain? He leaned forward, blew out the candle and lay back upon his bed.

'God, I don't know if You hear or even if You care, but I need to know the truth; the truth about You, about myself and why we are born to die.'

As the days passed, Costas's thoughts turned more and more to Melina. She was fresh as a spring day, gentle and kind. A smile crossed his lips. His mother had been trying to interest him in finding a wife, but none of the girls had appealed to him. He chuckled. In the end, he had found his future wife without the help of a matchmaker.

On Saturday afternoon, Costas and his parents ambled up the path to Melina's house. Costas was dressed in a brown suit with his hair slicked down, except for a stray wave that refused to lie flat. Nervously he straightened his tie, coughed, then knocked on the door. Melina's father answered the door. 'Welcome, welcome. Come in.'

After the formalities for an arranged marriage were completed satisfactorily between the parents, Melina's mother left the room. 'They're here, my dear.'

'Oh Mummy, I'm so frightened.'

'Nonsense. You look lovely and Costas is your friend. You don't need to be afraid. Now hold your head up and smile. That's better. Take the tray in and just be yourself.'

As Melina entered the door, Costas's mother caught her breath. Melina smiled shyly. Her hair, pulled away from her face, fell in ringlets down her back. She wore a green dress, fitted at the waist, with a full skirt that made a soft swishing sound as she walked. The green of her dress brought out the green highlights in her eyes and Costas thought he had never seen her look so enchanting.

12

The Party

Ali ripped open the envelope carelessly, but his eyes lit up as he realised the card was from his friend Costas whom he had met at university.

He could remember the day he had met Costas as though it were yesterday, although it was two years ago. Three youths had decided to beat him up. While he was desperately struggling on the ground with the three on top of him, he heard a tremendous roar. He chuckled now to think of it. Costas had ploughed into their midst, so taking them by surprise that within minutes they were racing away down the lane.

'Hi. Are you all right? My name is Costas.' He had extended his hand, and helped Ali up.

'Thanks, I'm Ali. For a minute there I thought the sky was falling.'

Costas chuckled. 'Ah, my friend, victory lies in the element of surprise!' The two boys laughed and from that day a bond had grown between them that no religious barriers could suppress.

So Costas is getting engaged! Ali smiled as he read the card.

It would be good to see Costas again; to be able to share his thoughts and know that even though he knew he could not face the engagement party when he was so discouraged, Costas would understand.

Several days later, Ali was sitting gloomily in his room. There was the sound of footsteps outside, and then Aysha knocked on the door.

'Ali, I have to talk to you.' Aysha was a breath of fresh air in Ali's darkened life. At the moment, she was his only source of comfort. 'Ali,' Aysha sat down, caught her breath, then spoke with excitement; 'Ali, I've seen Silvana.'

Ali perked up immediately, transformed from his previous despair to an acute and sharp awareness. 'How did she look? Is she well? Did she talk about me?'

'Hold on, hold on, let me tell you everything from the beginning.' Ali leaned forward, listening intently.

'Ali, she was going to meet you at the post office, but her father stopped her.'

'Oh –' Ali jumped to his feet, 'I knew it – I knew she wanted to marry me!' Ali walked across the room and threw his arms into the air, 'I knew it – yes, yes, yes!' His voice rose to a triumphant shout; 'Silvana, I love you!'

Aysha smiled. A warmth flooded her heart, and for a moment her eyes filled with tears as she saw this tormented soul released from part of the burden he was carrying.

'But what can I do, Aysha?' Ali's joy turned to more realistic thoughts. 'What can I do?'

Aysha reached out her hand and touched Ali on the arm. She looked down towards the floor, hesitated, then spoke. 'There is a problem. She is being forced to marry an older man whom she despises.'

Ali stood up and paced nervously up and down the room. Lifting his arms futilely in the air, the words seemed torn from him; 'Perhaps she will be happy.'

'But Ali, that man is just a dirty old man. He doesn't want to love her, or care for her; he just wants a toy to play with.'

'When is she to be married?'

Aysha looked at the floor again. 'In two weeks' time.'

Ali sighed loudly, then crumpled on to the chair. He closed his eyes, breathing heavily, then squeezed his eyes shut even tighter. 'What can we do? What can we do?'

Aysha got up and walked across to the window. Then softly but with determination, she said, 'We can pray.'

'Pray? What good will that do?'

'God is greater than any problem, Ali. He loves you and wants you to reach out to Him.'

Ali laughed bitterly. 'That's old woman's talk, Aysha.'

'No, it isn't,' Aysha responded firmly. 'I know, because God has helped me. I brought you something to read. It's about God.'

'That's not our Holy Book.' said Ali, looking suspiciously at the slim black book.

'Ali, you are so narrow-minded. You sit here

moaning about your fate as if it were already decided, already written down. Nothing is written; you choose what is written – what your fate will be. Why don't you stop feeling sorry for yourself and try doing something for a change?'

Ali shrugged his shoulders, surprised by her enthusiasm. 'All right. I have nothing left to lose, so why not?'

Melina was pleased to receive a visit from her friend. 'Hello, Silv. Do come in, I've been wanting to talk to you.'

The girls went to Melina's room and after chatting for a while, Melina came to the point. 'Silvana, seeing your unhappiness has upset me so much that I began to think about life, about the unfair things that just seem to happen for no reason, and also about God . . . Is God really what we imagine Him to be, demanding and even cruel? Costas has been a help to me, because he too has been concerned about such issues. He gave me a book that I've grown to love. Through reading it, I have realised that God does care about us and that He longs to help us in our troubles. I have asked Him to be the Lord of my life, and I've asked Him to use me to help you to find peace.'

Silvana shifted uneasily in her seat, ignoring the book that Melina held out to her.

'Melina, you are such a good friend and I love you the way you are. But don't you think you are getting extreme in your thoughts about God? What I mean is, it's okay to go to church once in a while, but surely we don't have to be so serious about religion?'

'What I'm talking about is more than religion. Religion can never satisfy. I'm talking about knowing God personally and learning to love Him.'

'Oh Melina, surely loving a man is much more relevant to life than loving a God we can't see! All I'm concerned about is being forced to marry a man I despise when I long to marry Ali. God doesn't enter my thoughts except when I think how unfair He is to me. Really, I have no time for God.'

The day of Melina's engagement party dawned bright and clear. She woke to the sun filtering through her curtains and the sound of a lark singing. It was good to be alive. She picked up her Holy Book, which she kept on the table by her bed, and began to read. 'Do not be anxious about anything, but in everything, by prayer and petition, with thanksgiving, present your requests to God. And the peace of God, which transcends all understanding, will guard your hearts and your minds in Christ Jesus.'

The peace of God is such a precious gift! she thought. Oh, that Silvana might come to understand that this peace could dwell in her heart, too!

Her door opened. 'Good morning, my dear. It's a perfect day for your party.'

Melina jumped out of bed and impetuously gave her mother a big hug. 'Oh Mamma, I love you so much.'

'I love you too, my precious.' Tears came into her mother's eyes and she brusquely wiped them away. 'But now come along, breakfast is ready and there is much to do.'

The time passed swiftly and in the early afternoon Costas and his parents arrived, followed by a number of their friends.

The only blot on the joy of the day for Melina was the thought that Silvana would never experience such happiness if her marriage to Mavramati became a reality. For Costas, it was that his dear friend Ali had not been able to share in his joy.

As Costas placed the ring on Melina's finger signifying their engagement, Melina felt that her heart would burst with joy. Costas was a kind young man, and together they shared a love for the same God. She looked forward to their marriage in the early autumn; and Costas, looking down at Melina, felt as if God had bestowed a very special treasure on him in the form of this delicate young girl by his side.

13

Wedding Day

As Silvana turned over in her bed, the awesome reality hit her that today she would be joined to Stavros Mavramati in marriage. In her mind, she had tried to block out the fact that this day would ever come. Now, however, it was here; and the harsh reality of its presence caused a feeling of despair to engulf her. A chill shuddered inside her, despite the warm sunlight that tumbled joyfully through the window in her room.

She rolled over and stared blankly across the room. 'Oh Ali,' she sobbed, 'I don't know where you are and I need you. Today I am to become another man's wife. Oh, if only you could save me from this day!'

After crying hopelessly for a while, she found herself praying. 'God? God, if You really do care, then please, please help me.'

Her thoughts were interrupted by her mother coming into the room, holding the wedding dress. Seeing her daughter lying there, so pale and numbed by pain, deeply grieved her.

'I'm sure it will work out all right.' Her mother

faltered for words in an attempt to comfort, but her words merely seemed to fall on to the carpet before her. Silvana turned and looked pleadingly at her mother. 'Mamma,' she began, but emotion overcame her and, collapsing back on to the bed, she began to cry helplessly. Her mother sat beside her and gently stroked her hair as if she were a small child. Then slowly, gathering her composure, Silvana sat up again.

'Mamma, I will try to be brave for your sake, but I know marriage to Stavros Mavramati will never bring me anything but unhappiness.'

Mavramati was already dressed for the wedding. A strong smell of day-old garlic clung about him. His brother, who had come into town specially for the wedding, stood at the other end of the room. 'Stavros,' his brother said seriously, 'you do see that this wedding is different from the other one, don't you?'

Mavramati turned and looked at his brother with disdain. What did his brother know about life, people, success or survival? 'What do you mean?' he sneered.

'This girl is very young; she is innocent and kind. You have an opportunity to share things with her, to show some kindness to someone for the first time in your life.'

Mavramati walked over to the mirror to admire himself, smiling at his reflection. The slimy appearance of his greasy skin accentuated his yellow, almost greenish, teeth. He reached into his pocket for a

used cigar, took his time lighting it, and then spoke.
'Dogs, that's what they are – dogs! You can pet
them, enjoy them, beat them when they don't obey
you, but you can never, never treat them as if they
are humans.' He turned his back towards his brother.
'She will be fine as long as she is as obedient as a dog;
she can even have happiness if she obeys me.' He
walked across to the table by the window and flicked
cigar ash into an ashtray. 'If she doesn't learn to
obey my every wish, she will be unhappy; very, very
unhappy.'

Silvana stood in front of the mirror; her large brown
eyes portrayed a mixture of pain and innocence. Her
shiny hair was bunched into ringlets high on her
head, giving her an almost royal appearance. Her full
lips, touched with lipstick, trembled; and from time
to time she bit her lower lip to keep from crying.

'It's time to go. Come along now,' her father called
impatiently.

Silvana felt physical pain as she thought of Ali.
How she wished that it was him she was going to
meet in the church! Instead, in her mind she could
picture Mavramati's sneering face drawing close to
her own; and fear clutched her heart.

'I said come along now.' Her father's impatience
intensified. 'We have to stop for Melina, hurry!'

The car that was to carry her to the church was
black. She imagined she was in a coffin slowly being
carried to its resting place. For her the church, rather
than being a place of spiritual birth, would be the
place that set the seal on her death; a death that

would carry her into the very mouth of hell itself.

As the car made its way through the streets, Silvana thought that everything around her seemed to be moving in slow motion. A man selling oranges from a barrow seemed to be shouting into a vast emptiness, his voice echoing from an immense distance.

After a few moments, they stopped at Melina's door. Melina was to be the bridesmaid. She got into the front seat and then turned to smile encouragingly at Silvana behind her.

'God will help you, Silv. I have been praying that somehow God would intervene. If He doesn't, I know He will give you strength to face each day, if you will only trust Him.'

The car slowly made its way towards the church. In the distance, Silvana could see a gathering of people.

Standing on the edge of the crowd she could see Mavramati isolated except for the presence of his brother. A wave of nausea swept over her. The moment she had dreaded was about to become a reality. The contract, which in the eyes of the world would mean a never-ending union binding two people together, was about to be sealed by a priest's words and the signing of a civil document.

Silvana's eyes narrowed in anger. She whispered, her lips barely moving, as she looked across the crowd to Stavros Mavramati, 'You may have a marriage document which allows you to take my body, you may even force your will upon me, but never will you have my heart, for it belongs to another.'

At the last moment, Ali had decided to come to the church with Costas, and now stood discreetly to one side so that he could see Silvana for one last time.

He watched eagerly as the large car came slowly towards the junction. But, suddenly, he was horrified to see a truck hurtling down a side street, careering across the junction.

There were screams, the squeal of tyres, and the harsh sound of metal grinding against metal as the left side of the car was struck right along its length. Everyone stood stunned as if it were a nightmare. Then, almost simultaneously, Costas and Ali raced up the street to the wreckage. 'Oh God help us,' gasped Costas. 'These doors won't open. Quick, Ali, let's try the other side.'

Racing to the other side of the car, with an almost super-human effort they were able to open the doors. With apparent calm, Costas coaxed Silvana's stunned parents, who though badly bruised were still conscious, out of the car. 'That's right, carefully now, come along, let us help you,' he said, at the same time gently lifting and supporting Silvana's father.

Ali helped Silvana's mother to the kerb, and looked desperately over to the crowd of onlookers, who seemed paralysed with shock. 'Quickly! These people need help.'

Tenderly Costas reached across the front seat and lifted Melina's broken, bleeding form out of the car. Meanwhile Ali carefully lifted Silvana, the tears streaming down his face.

Melina's parents had been inside the church when the accident occurred. Now, though filled with fear, they were able to bring some order to the chaos. Melina's father barked orders. 'Get a vehicle here, quickly! We've got to get the girls to the hospital. Come on!'

Melina's mother bent over her daughter and then Silvana, trying to stop the bleeding and to see that both were still alive.

Within minutes, a van pulled up to the kerb. Rapidly the girls, both unconscious, were lifted into the waiting vehicle.

'Hurry! Their lives depend on it. God go with us!' said Melina's father brokenly as he got into the van.

Another car pulled up and Silvana's parents were helped into it.

As the car pulled away, Ali slumped to the ground. 'Oh God – help! They are dying. Silvana is dying!'

'Come on, Ali. Get up,' urged Costas. 'Sitting there won't help anyone. They might need us at the hospital. I only pray that the doctor is there now. Come on, let's go.'

As the girls were carried into the hospital and laid on stretchers, Doctor Sofianu shook his head in despair. 'They are both in a critical condition and I can only operate on one at a time.'

'Doctor.' He was astonished to hear a faint whisper from Melina's lips. He leaned down to hear more clearly. 'Doctor, take care of my friend first. Please. She needs you most.'

'No!' The cry of anguish seemed to be torn from the depths of her father's being. 'No, you may die if he does that.'

'I know, Daddy. Please, Doctor, please. I'm ready to die. Silvana isn't.'

'Okay, my child, don't fret. I will do my best.' The doctor was relieved that he did not have to make the decision as to who should live or who might ultimately die. Melina lapsed back into unconsciousness.

Doctor Sofianu spoke to the nurse. 'We need blood quickly. We must find some suitable donors.'

The nurse walked into the lobby, now filled with relatives and close friends.

'We need blood. Would some of you be willing to help us?' Many nodded. Quickly the nurse set about taking blood samples and then did a simple test to see whose blood was compatible with that of the girls.

Meanwhile, Costas and Ali had joined Melina's father in the emergency room. 'Doctor, is there anything we can do?'

'Yes, get two stretchers and put one beside each girl. Nurse, get needles and tubing. We will start by putting the blood directly from the donors into the girls. Have you found suitable donors?'

'Yes, Melina's mother and a Mr Philipou have suitable blood. They are ready and waiting.'

'Good. Prepare for surgery, nurse.' The doctor spoke grimly as he worked quickly and quietly, telling the two donors to lie down and beginning the transfusion first on Silvana and then on Melina.

'I have called the city hospital. They are sending us help,' the nurse said, then bustled off to the operating theatre and began to prepare for surgery.

Twenty minutes later Silvana was wheeled into the operating room.

When a relief doctor and a nurse finally arrived from the city hospital, they found Melina still in the emergency room, struggling for breath.

'I'm afraid we may be too late,' the doctor murmured softly when he had examined her.

'What did you say?' Costas asked with disbelief and horror in his voice.

The doctor glanced at Costas as he began to work. 'She is dying. I can only do my best. In cases like this, an immediate operation is the only hope. Find out if they have a second operating room.'

Within minutes Costas was back. 'No, Doctor. Only the one that is already in use, and they will be at least another hour,'

'If we don't operate immediately, she is certain to die. Nurse, get the basic equipment we need to operate here.'

As they moved the equipment into place, the doctor looked curiously at Costas.

'Young man, who are you?'

'I am Melina's fiancé.'

'Well, I need your help. Do you think you will be able to cope with what you will see?'

Nervously, Costas nodded his head. 'With God's help, I will, sir.' Silently Costas breathed a prayer as fear seemed to clutch his stomach. 'I think I'll be all right,' he said, taking a deep breath.

'Good. I'll tell you exactly what to do. You will help me give the anaesthetic. Now, let's get to work.'

During the next hour Costas concentrated harder than he ever had in his life. Sweat poured off him as he followed the doctor's instructions. Eventually Dr Sofianu appeared, looking tired and haggard. 'How is it going?'

'Not so well, but she's still alive. How is your patient?'

'She should be okay, God willing. Only time will tell.'

Sofianu left the room again and the work went on. Costas had lost count of the time when, at last, the operation was finished and Melina was ready to be wheeled into another room. Costas and the doctor lifted her on to the bed. The doctor tested her pulse and blood pressure once again. He sighed, and Costas looked at him anxiously.

'You have been very helpful. But it's better that you should know the truth.'

Costas looked at the ground, and then at the doctor. Truth! he thought; yes, he wanted to hear the truth, but most of all he wanted to hear the doctor say that Melina would be fine and that there was nothing to worry about. He wanted to hear those words no matter what; he nodded to the doctor, 'Yes, yes, please tell me.'

'Her injuries are very serious. Only God can help her now.'

Costas stared in disbelief. 'You don't mean she is dying?'

'Yes, I'm afraid so. You will need to be strong. Her parents will need your support.' The doctor placed his hand on Costas's shoulder briefly, then went out of the room.

Costas sank to his knees beside the bed, took Melina's limp hand in his own and began to weep.

As he knelt by the bed, a picture flashed into his mind of the time he had first noticed Melina. She was seven years old and he was ready to take on the world at the lofty age of nine.

He and his family had come to Melina's house to

pay a visit. Melina had been given a sand-coloured kitten for her birthday. A wandering dog had seen it and given chase. The frightened kitten had taken refuge in the great cedar tree in the garden and had not stopped climbing until it reached the top. Melina, in distress, had tried to coax the kitten down but nothing would cause it to budge from its place of safety. After a while the kitten had begun to mew piteously. Melina, her heart touched by the plight of her kitten, had begun bravely to climb the old tree. When she had reached the kitten and held it safely in her arms, she had smiled contentedly, unaware of how high she had climbed. As she looked down, the ground had seemed miles away. Clinging tightly to the kitten, she had tried to descend but found the next branch too far below her to reach while holding the kitten. At that point, she had begun to be quite frightened. Her cries for help had gone unheeded until Costas and his family arrived.

Sizing up the situation, the boy moved quickly and was soon seated beside the tearstained child. The sun had shone playfully through the leaves, causing the tears on Melina's lashes to sparkle. The sunlight fell on her dishevelled hair, picking up coppery highlights and framing the little face, smudged with dirt where she had rubbed it with a grimy little fist. As he sat in the tree beside her, he felt the desire to protect this plucky little mite from all danger. Tenderly, he had soothed her fears and then helped her and the kitten down to the ground. From that day he had been her champion.

Now, powerless to help her, he wept. The door opened and Melina's parents entered. Their eyes were swollen and red. Costas rose to his feet and embraced Melina's mother and then her father; then together they knelt around the bed and prayed that God would spare their beloved.

The three waited anxiously at her bedside. As time slid by, their anxiety heightened. Melina's father got up and nervously paced the room while Costas sat at the window staring into the darkness. Silently the tears slid down the mother's cheeks as she looked at her daughter, so pale and so still.

It seemed like hours later when a shaft of moonlight fell across the still form. It was almost as if the moon was trying to infuse life into the bruised body, lying so pale and deathlike. Then, to everyone's joy, Melina's fingers moved and she slowly opened her eyes.

'Melina, my precious baby!' Her mother leaned over and kissed her.

'Mamma.' Her fingers reached out to grasp her mother's hand. Melina's voice was very faint, yet she seemed composed, even happy.

'Mamma, Daddy, and Costas. How I love you all! God has been so good to me and I thank Him for each of you. I read a verse this morning. It said, "I am the resurrection and the life. He who believes in me will live, even though he dies."' Her mother tenderly patted her hand. 'I am dying.' Tears were streaming down the faces of the three at the bedside as they looked at the radiant face of their beloved Melina.

'God is love, and He is taking me home to be with Him, to live in His wonderful garden. One day you shall join me there and then He will wipe all tears from your eyes.'

Melina's eyes closed and her mother bent over her. 'My darling, my little one. Don't go yet! We love you.'

Melina's eyes fluttered open. 'Mamma,' she said, barely above a whisper, 'Mamma, give my New Testament to Silvana. Tell her I love her and that I have prayed that one day she will meet me in the garden, but she has to get ready if she wants to go there when she dies. I love you, Mamma,' her eyes lifted to her father, 'I love you, Papa,' her eyes focused on her fiancé, 'and I love you, Costas.' Her eyes lit up with joy and her face spread into a smile. 'I can hear music, Mamma. Jesus is calling me. Goodbye!'

Her eyes closed and her hand went limp. 'Melina, Melina. Don't go!' Her mother slumped, sobbing, over her daughter's body. Costas turned and raced blindly from the room, through the hospital and out into the night, unaware of Ali calling him.

As he wept, he found himself raising his voice in anger. 'Why, God? Why? Why Melina? She is beautiful and kind and has never hurt anyone. Why her?' Life was so cruel, so very unfair.

The night was silent. The stars continued to glisten almost like teardrops. Several hours passed unnoticed. Then, softly, with wonder, he spoke aloud. 'God, You care too, don't You? You weep with us. What was that Melina said? One day You will wipe all tears from our eyes. Oh God, give me faith to trust You, in spite of my pain, to see You as You are. I love You, God, and I trust You.' Though the tears continued to flow, there was a peace in his heart and an assurance that God makes no mistakes.

Back in the hospital, Silvana had begun to haemorrhage. Only one visitor remained seated in the lobby, his head in his hands.

'Excuse me.' The nurse's tired voice seemed to come from a long way away. 'Is your name Ali?' Ali looked up in confusion. 'We desperately need extra blood. Silvana is bleeding and we need to give her another transfusion. Your blood is suitable. Would you help us?'

At the mention of Silvana's name, Ali was out of his chair. 'Yes, please, I want to help.'

The nurse led Ali into the room where Silvana lay, Dr Sofianu working over her. Ali was instructed to lie on the stretcher placed beside the bed. Quickly a needle was inserted into his vein, tubing was connected to this with a second needle at the other end, which was then inserted into Silvana's arm. Slowly the life-saving blood flowed from Ali into Silvana's body.

Half an hour later Dr Sofianu spoke. 'I think she has a chance now. Her lips are no longer blue. But she needs more blood. What do you think, son? It's up to you. If you give any more blood it is going to leave you quite weak.'

'No, don't think about me. She is the one who needs the blood. Take whatever she needs.'

Sometime later Silvana moaned and grasped at her covers in agitation. 'Ali, I need you. Oh, I have to marry that evil man,' she moaned. In distress, she began to toss and turn in the bed.

'We must calm her or her life will be in danger,' the doctor said hoarsely.

A tear slid down Ali's cheek as he looked at Silvana.

. Taking a deep breath, he spoke from his stretcher. 'Silvie, it's me, Ali. Listen to me. Everything is going to be all right. I am here now. There isn't going to be a wedding.' Ali's voice soothed her and in minutes Silvana lay quietly. The doctor nodded, satisfied, and disconnected the tubing.

An orderly helped Ali to another room. 'Here, drink this juice. You need the extra liquid as you've lost so much blood. You may rest here for the night.' Gratefully Ali relaxed on the bed and, in minutes, sleep mercifully overtook him.

Three days later, a grief-stricken community attended Melina's funeral. Many had wailed their grief, but all were touched by the hopefulness shown by Melina's parents and fiancé, in spite of the deep grief they were experiencing.

Costas had read from the little black book that Melina had treasured. 'These words, which Jesus spoke, were some of the last words on Melina's lips.

'"I am the resurrection, and the life. He who believes in me, will live, even though he dies; and whoever lives and believes in me will never die."

'Today, Melina is alive in God's garden. Those who accept the One whom Melina loved as Lord will one day see her again; that is our blessed hope.'

14

Insights

In the days since the accident, Ali had spent many anxious moments hovering outside Silvana's room.

'Who are you?'

Startled out of his thoughts, Ali looked up to see Silvana's father standing over him, his head bandaged and his arm held in a sling.

'They told me you helped rescue my daughter from the wreck and that you gave blood so she might live. I owe you a lot. What is your name?'

'I'm Ali.'

'Ali? Not that Muslim boy my daughter intended to run off with?' His voice rose with anger.

'We were going to be married, sir. We love each other.'

'Love!' Petros spat with disgust. 'What do you know about love?'

Ali did not answer. Petros glared at him. Yet, as he noticed the young man's face, filled with pain, the sleepless eyes, the rumpled hair, several days' stubble on the chin, and the hands clasping and unclasping in a futile expression of helplessness, his anger suddenly fizzled away. Yes, this boy did love his daughter. That was obvious to all.

Petros turned away, hesitated, then turned back to Ali. 'She is still unconscious. Would you like to see her? The doctor thinks she will die. Maybe if you talk to her...' His voice trailed off as he turned and re-entered the room.

Silvana's mother was sitting in a chair by the bedside, a rumpled tissue in her hand which she used from time to time to wipe a tear away and at which she picked restlessly. Ali nodded to her, but her eyes were vacantly focused on her daughter's face. The uniformed nurse beside her looked suspiciously at him.

As he walked over to the side of the bed and saw the unconscious form of the girl he loved, a ball of pain hit him in the pit of his stomach, and he began to weep.

'Silvie, it's me, Ali. Everything is going to be all right now. Silvie, open your eyes. Silvie, I need you. Don't give up.'

'I'm sorry, but you will have to leave.' The nurse spoke coldly. 'Only immediate relatives are allowed in the room.'

Dejectedly, Ali got up. 'Goodbye, Mr Silvanou. Thank you.'

He found himself walking aimlessly through the town. Tired and discouraged, he decided to visit Costas.

'Ali! How are you? Come in. You look like you need a rest. Come along and have a warm bath and then try to sleep.' Costas led the way into their modest bathroom.

'How is Silvana?'

'She's still unconscious. The doctor says she will probably die.'

'That's rough. We must keep praying.'

Once Ali's head hit the pillow, he drifted immediately off to sleep. The sound of a cockerel woke him. Groggily he staggered to the bathroom and splashed cold water on his face. He found Costas having breakfast.

'Good morning! You must have slept well; you look much better. How do you feel?'

Ali nodded. 'Better, thanks.'

Costas seemed to have pulled his life together, despite the fact that the girl he loved had died so tragically, Ali thought to himself. What was it about this man that he could be calm in the midst of such pain? He had to ask.

'Costas, you watched the girl you love die. Yet you are so brave, so peaceful. Seeing Silvana lying so pale and motionless was such a shock. I thought after that night I gave her blood, that, well, that she was going to get better. But she's no different. Still, there is a chance that she might live. But for Melina there is no chance. I hope you don't mind me asking but I don't understand.'

Costas smiled. 'No, it's all right, I don't mind. You are right. We have a similar pain in common. Although I feel deep pain, I know that one day I will see Melina in heaven; that is what gives me hope.'

For a brief moment, Ali felt again the emotion he had experienced earlier when sitting alone looking at the candle in his room. 'Heaven? What do you mean? Do you believe we live on after we die?' A new vitality came into his voice as he questioned Costas.

'I do.' Costas looked serious, then smiled. 'Yes, I really do. Not a fairy-tale kind of heaven, but a real place with God as a friend who cares and who loves to be with His people.'

Ali hunched his shoulders and walked across the room, trying not to appear as excited as he felt. Costas continued, 'You see, I know this will be hard for you to accept, but the Bible teaches that man tries to reach up to God by religious rituals and rules, yet always falls short of God. So God in His love has reached down to man.'

Ali looked up, startled, and grabbed Costas's arm. 'What?! Reached down to man? Costas, tell me again slowly. What do you mean? I can't even begin to tell you how important this is to me. I was on a hill and there was a mosque and a cathedral and, oh – I'll tell you later; just tell me what you mean by God reaching down to man.'

Costas looked closely at Ali's expression. 'I can't tell you all in one shot; your whole background will rebel against it.'

'Costas,' Ali looked pleadingly at his friend. 'What are you? A drug pusher holding back on a junkie? I desperately need to know. I've been going out of my mind because life is futile and has no meaning. So tell me, will you?'

Costas laughed. 'I'm sorry, I just wanted to be sensitive. What we believe is almost always decided by our background, our parents, their parents, their religious background and – well, you know what I mean. So when we hear an idea different to what we have been taught, we automatically put up all the questions and arguments that our parents would have done, without really thinking over what we have heard. That makes it hard to examine new ideas in an honest way.'

'Okay, okay, I hear you.' Ali looked impatient. 'Just tell me what you believe about God reaching down to man.'

Costas smiled; a friendly, wholesome smile. Putting his hand on Ali's shoulder, he said, 'Let's go for a walk. I'll try to give it to you straight, right from the beginning, but it's not going to be quick.'

Once outside, Ali turned and faced his friend. 'Costas, losing Silvana's love, and then seeing her lying there so helpless is difficult, but it is only part of my problem. It merely seems to have taken the lid off my emotions. I am desperate to know the truth about God.'

Costas looked thoughtful as his friend spoke, nodded, smiled reassuringly, and then carried on walking.

The sun was shining and there was a freshness about the day as the two walked down the long winding pathway through the centre of the park.

'Ali, God is seen through so many eyes. Our view of God is almost totally tied into what religion our parents have, our culture, and even our country. That's why we find it hard to look at facts without our background, or even without history influencing our decisions. But try and divorce your mind from everything that you know and listen with an open mind.'

'Okay, I'll try.' Ali looked serious. 'Although I suppose we can never escape from history.'

Costas continued; 'The Bible teaches that God made man out of the dust of the ground and that he was different from all the animals.'

Ali frowned. 'What do you mean?'

'God created the animals already living. However, Adam only became a living soul when God breathed the breath of life into his nostrils. Man's very existence as a person was dependent upon something of God being breathed into his life. God and man were totally at one with each other. When Adam sinned, something terrible happened. His body still lived, but the perfection that God had breathed into him was destroyed and God and man were no longer linked in that close, intimate, spiritual way. Since then, all men have been separated from God.'

Ali looked intently at Costas. 'What you are saying is incredibly deep.'

Costas smiled. 'I know. But the important thing is that God never created man to be His slave. He made Adam to be His friend, and He was his friend until Adam sinned and turned his back on God. Man rejected God; God has never rejected man. Since then, down through history, man has tried to force God to be united with him by observing various religious rituals, supposedly to please God.'

Ali interrupted, 'You can't be saying that all these religions are merely ways man tries to force God to do what he wants?'

'I don't think it necessarily is a conscious thought where one says, "God, if I pray, give alms to the poor – " or something like that, "then You will do what I want." I think it's more complicated. It's as if man knows that he is cut off from God; something inside him is empty...'

Ali nodded. 'I know the feeling.'

'...and so to fill that emptiness, he is always trying to reach out to God.' Costas raised his voice a little in excitement. 'But you and I both know that following the prescribed patterns of our religions, reaching out to God, causes us nothing but frustration. No matter how hard we try, we can never reach Him.'

Ali nodded in agreement. 'Yes, I know. One evening, I stood on a hill from which I could see both a mosque and a cathedral. It struck me that here are two religions, both convinced they are right. Each is convinced their way of reaching out to God is the only way, yet neither group ever reaches God. But tell me, you said that God reached down to man. How does He do that?'

'God has always understood our problems and so He took the step to reach down to man in Jesus Christ.'

Ali smiled. 'We also believe Jesus was a prophet.'

'That is good, but I believe Jesus was greater than just a prophet...'

Ali looked nervous. 'What is so different about Jesus Christ from all the other prophets?'

Costas smiled. 'This is where you are going to struggle with history, the religion of our parents, and our cultural problem.'

'Come on Costas, that is fine for you. You have been brought up as a Christian. But I could never believe the way you do.'

'Don't you see, Ali, that I'm not talking about

candles and icons – I'm talking about a personal faith in God.'

'Yeah, that's great. But it sounds like you're trying to get me to change my religion. Let me think about what you've said. I need to go now.'

Ali had been able to get a job at the local factory so that he could stay in the city near Silvana. He rented a cheap room in an apartment house, and went there only to fall exhausted into his bed to sleep.

For weeks he spent every spare moment at the hospital. Mr Silvanou, touched by Ali's faithfulness, occasionally allowed him to visit Silvana's room for a few moments. Watching her life quietly ebbing away, leaving her pale and fragilely transparent, filled her father's heart with despair. Having Ali to share in his sorrow was a small comfort to him. Even though a bond began to grow unawares between them, they were still reserved in their acceptance of each other.

15

Questions

The crowded street seemed to be a mad fanfare of noise and activity. Costas had arranged to meet Ali at noon at the café. The piece of paper in Ali's pocket symbolised more than just a series of questions written on it, for the last days had been days of immense searching. The whole question of a caring God had been much in his mind. He felt so helpless seeing Silvana lying so still. Though he longed to use his strength to fight on her behalf, he knew he was powerless to snatch her from the clutches of death.

As he walked slowly towards the café to meet Costas, he tried to imagine facing life without her. The thought caused him to quicken his step – almost as if he were trying to escape from such thoughts.

Costas was sitting in the corner at a table set for two. He waved to Ali, who made his way through the busy comings and goings at the front entrance.

'Ali, you look tired. How is Silvana today?' Costas's clear and genuinely interested gaze gave Ali a feeling of comfort.

'Not so good. I don't think I can stand much more of this.' Ali pounded his fist on the table. 'I feel so inadequate, it makes me angry.'

After the waiter had taken their order, Ali looked across at Costas with a pondering look. 'Well, Costas, I must admit you made an impression on me the other day during our talk.' He hesitated for a moment and then unfolded the piece of paper that was in his pocket. 'I have done a tremendous amount of thinking and I've written down some questions I have. Think about them and then let's talk again, rather than you trying to answer them here and now.'

Costas nodded, taking the paper. Sipping his tea, he then looked at Ali. 'God loves you, Ali. It is no accident that we became friends.'

Ali looked nervous, 'I, ah, well, I don't know. I'm sure it was either fate or a coincidence.'

Costas looked at his watch. 'Hey, I'm going to be late for work! I'll see you tomorrow up at the park, okay? Meanwhile, I'll look at these questions.' He smiled, then rushed off towards the door.

Ali watched his friend leave, and then called the waiter over to order more tea. The noise in the café seemed to drift into the background as he pondered the words Costas had said. *God loves you.* Was it possible that God could actually love him?

The sun had just risen over the city and the blending together of the deep oranges and yellows in a fan-like shape around the sun gave a peaceful yet expectant atmosphere to the day.

The park where Ali and Costas were to meet seemed to be waking out of sleep, with the occasional squirrel darting in and out of the trees. There was a large twisted tree that seemed ageless. The twisting, arching, almost strained form of nature gave a solid and secure touch to the otherwise fresh and new atmosphere of the park. The trees were changing their dress. From their summer's green to joyous colours of red and gold they transformed the woodland into a riot of colour. A gentle wisp of wind occasionally rustled through the leaves, and every now and then, a mischievous leaf tumbled and twirled through the air until it reached the ground. The carpet of leaves, reflecting the beauty overhead, combined with the unusual mildness of the early-morning weather, created a hopeful element for the meeting of Ali and Costas.

Ali was wearing jeans and a rumpled shirt. His face, darkened by several days' growth of beard, was drawn and tense; his eyes were heavy from lack of sleep. Costas was wearing smart denims and a blue suede jacket with a chequered shirt under it. As they walked towards the hill that overlooked the rose gardens, both were aware that some intense questioning had been taking place in Ali's mind.

'I've read the list of questions.' Costas smiled but kept walking, looking up at the sky with its heralding of the new day.

Ali turned towards his friend. 'What do you think? Can you answer them?'

'Sure, sure I can answer them, but I don't really know if they are honest questions.'

Ali, slightly taken aback, stopped and then said,

'What do you mean?'

Costas smiled. 'I'm sorry, it's just that they are the standard questions which your parents and their parents would ask. I don't know if you have really thought things through for yourself.'

Ali smiled. 'Okay, let's talk about it.'

'First, you say the Bible has been changed, so how can you trust what it says? Ali, in England and in Israel they have manuscripts that date back to the first century, which prove it hasn't been changed. But more important is this; the God who can make the universe, create all living things, the incomprehensible God who is King of the ages, is powerful enough to stop His revelation from being destroyed. It is impossible that God would have let His Word get changed.'

Ali looked closely at Costas. 'So, you don't want to argue from a logical standpoint even though you claim you can.'

'Logic is fine,' Costas replied, 'if you are willing to follow it through, but the issue is this; is my God big enough to stop His Word from being destroyed? Yes, my God is big enough.'

Ali stopped dead in his tracks. 'Well, how about the other questions? You know – God having a wife.'

'Ali, anyone who believes that God has taken a wife to Himself is guilty of blasphemy.' Costas looked annoyed. 'It's a dirty lie to say such things. The Bible teaches that God's Spirit came upon Mary, and without sexual union, she conceived a child in her womb, who was Jesus.'

Ali was visibly surprised. 'Does the Bible really teach that?'

'Yes, it does.'

'All right. Well, how about Jesus dying on the cross? If God is so powerful, He could never let His prophet die in such a way. That's why God placed Jesus' likeness on someone else, who was crucified in His place. Answer that one then!'

Costas placed his hand on Ali's shoulder. 'The Bible teaches that God would have sent thousands of angels to destroy those who were hurting Jesus, if Jesus had asked. But you see, He never asked. All the angels in heaven drew their swords ready to protect Jesus but God said, "No, wait, there is a plan. There is a reason why all this is happening."

'You know, God speaks to man in ways he can understand. God made a covenant with Abraham, where He promised to be Abraham's God. For centuries the highest type of agreement that two people could make was known as "the cutting of a covenant". It was used between tribal chiefs who wished to make peace or between two people who wished to demonstrate their love and commitment to each other.

'First came the formal ceremony in which they exchanged clothing, weapons, and names; thus pledging themselves to each other. Blessings would be promised to those honouring the convenant and a curse promised to the one who broke the covenant. Then came the rite of the shedding of blood, where each would cut himself. They would then mingle their blood together. As a "seal" on this they rubbed something such as ash into the wounds leaving a permanent scar as a continual reminder of the covenant.'

'That's all very interesting, but I don't see what it has to do with my question.'

'Let me continue. Circumcision was the cutting God requested of Abraham and of every male in his family. When Abraham was circumcised, it was the visible reminder of God's covenant to him.'

'So that's why circumcision is important. Hmm. Hey, wait a minute. Haven't you forgotten something?'

'What do you mean?'

'Well, if both had to cut themselves, what did God do to cut Himself?'

Costas smiled. 'God had His feet and hands pierced by nails and had a sword thrust into His side when Jesus died on the cross.'

'That's hard to believe.' Ali frowned.

'Maybe, but isn't it harder to believe that God did not have enough honour to allow Himself to be cut in fulfilment of His part of the covenant? And how could God be cut in a visible way, unless He became a man? Don't you see, Ali? Jesus had to die. He couldn't let another take His place.'

Ali paced nervously up and down. Abruptly he turned. 'I want to be on my own,' he said, then strode rapidly away.

16

The Dream

Ali sat cross-legged on the floor in his parents'
home with the Bible he had just purchased placed
carefully on a little table in front of him. The words
that he read were so powerful that they seemed to cut
their way into the innermost areas of his being like a
knife.

As he began to read the story about a wayward
son, his heart beat with anger. The youngest son
went to his father demanding his inheritance. It was
like saying, 'I wish you were dead, Father. Give me
what will be mine when you die.'

Instead of the father severely punishing his son for
his disrespect he did an unheard-of thing; he gave the
boy his inheritance. The son quickly sold all his share
of land and animals and, taking the money, left home.
In a far-away country, he had many friends as he
lived in luxury, wasting his money. Then famine hit
the land and his money was soon gone. Destitute, his
friends gone, the only job he could get was the lowly

job of caring for pigs. As he became weak with hunger, he was even tempted to eat some of the husks the pigs were eating.

Coming to his senses, he realised his father's servants had food to spare and here he sat starving. 'I will go home and ask my father to take me as his servant, so I won't starve.' He arose and walked the long journey home, preparing a speech for when he would see his father.

His father spent every spare moment on the roof-top searching the countryside. 'Surely one day my son will return to me!' Then one morning, as he looked over the countryside, his eyes lit upon a bent figure in the distance. His heart leapt. 'Can this be my son?' The figure drew near the edge of the village. The father cried with joy. 'It is! It is my son!' The elderly man lifted his robes and hurried down the stairs.

Meanwhile, at the edge of the village, the son had paused. He knew there would be punishment by the villagers for the disrespect he had shown his father. Thoughts of the tauntings and curses, the stones that would be hurled at him, and the shame of every footstep he would have to take through the village struck fear into his heart. Noise broke through his thoughts, for he heard a great commotion in the village. Then, to his utter amazement, he recognised his father running down the road, his robes lifted like a youth's. The villagers were running alongside him mocking and jeering. No respectable man, and certainly never an elderly man, would be seen running.

Stunned, the young man realised his father was coming to meet him, and knowing the shame of the

path his son would walk to reach home, had willingly
taken that shame on himself to spare his son. Tears
began to stream down the son's face. He had come
home merely because he was hungry, but now he
understood that his father loved him very deeply,
and with a heart full of forgiveness, he was willing to
take his son's punishment. As the father threw his
arms about his ragged, filthy son, their tears mingled.
The son, broken by his father's love, could not deliver
his carefully prepared speech. Instead he humbly
asked his father's forgiveness. The father, instead of
punishing his unworthy son, responded in love,
clothing his son in his own best robe, and preparing a
feast for him.

In unbelief, Ali read the story again. It was too
wonderful to believe, and yet how his heart longed
for it to be a picture of what God was like!

Suddenly the door burst open, and his father came
into the room. 'So it *is* true. You are reading that
book! I can't believe this, Ali.'

Ali's father was a cultured man who had broken
away from the traditions of his family. Initially, he
had earned money by wrestling, but in his late teen-
age years he had learned to read and to write.
Acquiring a thirst for knowledge, he had gone on to
educate himself. Marrying into a cultured family, he
had slowly developed a good position in the
community. Now this was threatened by his son's
flirting with another religion.

Ali looked up at his father from his sitting position.
'I'm only reading, that's all.'

'That's all!' his father shouted. 'First you come
home brokenhearted because you want to marry an

unclean Christian woman, then you top it all with reading their Holy Book!

'Now listen carefully. I want you to take that book and wrap it in cloth, bind it twenty times, then go and bury it. When you have buried it you are to place a charm over it and cover it with soil. Then you are to spit on the ground where it is buried.'

Ali could hardly believe his ears. He got up from his cross-legged position and walked over to his father. 'I can't believe you, Father. Surely you don't believe in all that superstitious nonsense from village life, do you? You go and bury it. Here, take it.' He offered the book to his father, who stepped back quickly to avoid touching it.

Raising his hand in an almost defensive gesture, he spoke anxiously. 'I won't touch it. It's bad luck.'

Ali stood looking at his father in amazement. 'I will take the book out of your house, but I will not bury it. I see now that our response to this book does not come from loyalty to God, but rather stems from fear.'

Ali's father frowned almost pleadingly. 'Ali, it's not for us. It's not our religion, it's not our history. If my brothers find out about this, they will go wild. Do you remember me telling you about the day a foreigner came into our village with this book? A man in our village gave him hospitality and because of that, my brothers cut down his olive trees, which were his only source of livelihood.'

Ali looked on, puzzled by his father's agony. 'But surely those were the old days. This is the city; times are changing – people are different now. Can't we at least learn from other books?'

Ali's father bowed his head, then spoke grimly, his words sounding like a line from some melodramatic movie. 'Ali, some things never change.' He turned and stormed out of the room, slamming the door behind him.

Ali looked at the Bible he was holding in his hands. He thought of the story of the wayward son and the forgiving father. Slowly, the conviction that he must continue reading encompassed him. Surely there was more to life than to be held captive by superstition and fear!

The little pastry shop was less crowded than the last time Costas had met Ali there. A large carpet hung on the wall, supposedly depicting a scene from heaven. Costas thought to himself how different the carpet's picture of heaven, with its beautiful maidens, was from what the Bible taught.

He was brought back to the present by the waiter, asking for his order: 'Two teas, please.'

Costas looked closely at his friend as Ali began to speak. 'I've been thinking a lot about what we have been talking about; of God reaching down to us in Jesus Christ.' Ali fidgeted with his cup, then looked up. 'Well, I've decided that I now have no religion. Of course, I do on my identity card, but you know that my heart is an empty compartment that I want filled by God, and not by a religion. I will need time to think and to pray it all through on my own.'

Costas reached out, grasped his friend's shoulder and smiled. 'Ali, I don't want you to have my religion. That won't help you! But I do want you to have my

God. I will pray for you in your search, that you personally will find the truth for yourself. There is so much beauty in both our cultures. There is no need for either of us to reject our culture to be linked together in friendship. Also, God exists outside the realm of culture. May you find Him there!'

Ali smiled. 'Thank you, Costas. Will you also pray for Silvana, that she will live and will find faith in God? Even if we can't marry, she needs a purpose to live for.' Costas nodded. The waiter returned to clear the table and they ordered more tea and then sat in companionable silence, sipping.

That evening Ali sat in his little room thinking and reading. The flickering kerosene lamp, which made the shadows dance on the wall, had become associated with his searching for a God who was reaching down to man.

He continued to read late into the night, interested in spite of himself in the words of Jesus. His mind was tortured as he lay down upon his bed. His thoughts quickly jumped from Silvana, to Costas, and then Aysha. Then he found himself speaking out loud, almost as if he were trying to convince himself. 'I am my own person. Surely, I can separate myself from what I have been taught so I can seriously consider this Holy Book!'

As he drifted off to sleep, he began to dream. It was not a normal dream filled with jumbled ideas and people, but a dream that was clear, sharp, and precise. He dreamt that he stood once again upon the hill overlooking the city with its mosque and cathedral. As he looked down over the city, he saw an elderly man with a snowy-white beard and kindly, wrinkled face coming around the bend in the road. Somehow, without being told, he knew it was Abraham. As Abraham walked, he seemed to be looking in anticipation for someone.

Then another man appeared. Again, without being told, Ali knew it was God's messenger. 'The Messiah is coming! He is further down the road, but one day He shall appear as the Lamb of God who takes away the sin of the world.'

Abraham's face broke into a smile and, as he turned in joy, a crowd of people appeared and gathered around him. Ishmael, Isaac, and the rest of his family rejoiced with Abraham.

In the distance, Ali could see another man coming down the road. As he drew near, Ali realised he must be an important person, for the man, although young, was dressed in kingly robes.

Again, the messenger spoke. 'David! The King of all creation is going to come one day as a servant to be the Messiah.'

David leapt for joy and, taking a harp, began singing songs of praise to God.

Then, as Ali looked, yet another man appeared. In His face was great strength of character and yet there was something infinitely gentle and tender in His demeanour. Children and the animals and birds of the field followed Him, totally unafraid.

The messenger spoke, with great reverence and yet joy in his voice. 'Behold, the Lamb of God, the promised Messiah; Jesus, the Holy One of God.'

Abraham, David and a host of others gathered

around, singing and rejoicing. Then the Messiah raised His head. His eyes looked piercingly into Ali's. 'Ali, I am the Promised One. Why do you resist Me? I am the One you are searching for.'

Suddenly, Ali woke up. His room felt warm and familiar and he experienced no fear, despite the shock of the dream.

Looking around, he realised how excited he now was. 'Oh Allah, I see it now. It's so clear! Jesus is the One who was needed and who was predicted down through the ages. That's why Abraham rejoiced, because God revealed to him that Jesus would come to be the suffering, saving Messiah. Oh God, forgive me everything that is sinful in me. Fill my heart with Yourself.'

A deep awareness that he had done the right thing descended upon him. He was still Ali, son of his father, but now he was a new person, born afresh by God's Spirit.

In his new-found joy Ali spent many hours each day reading the Bible. He found within its pages the direction he had been seeking for his own life. As he read, he was amazed to find the Bible was vibrantly alive and totally relevant to the problems of a modern society.

Where he had previously just put in the necessary hours at his job, now he applied all his energy to do his very best, believing that this pleased God.

God had now become his dearest friend, to whom he confided all his problems. Often, in the late hours of the night, he found himself pouring out his agony and pent-up feelings about Silvana to God.

Then one night, feeling deeply sorry for himself,

he abstractedly flipped through the pages of his Bible until the Book fell open by itself. Looking down, his eyes fell on the verse, 'Give thanks in all circumstances, for this is God's will for you in Christ Jesus.'

'Give thanks, when the girl I love may die? No chance!'

With anger he closed the Book and stamped across the room, slamming the door as he left the house.

Outside a light rain was falling. The weather seemed to fit Ali's mood as he walked sullenly down the road, mulling over angry thoughts about the unfairness and cruelty of life. Persistently the words 'Give thanks in all circumstances' kept running like a thread through his thoughts. Kicking a stone out of his way he grumbled aloud, 'It's all right for You to say that, God, but let's be realistic. You don't really understand what it is to suffer. You have never experienced prejudice or hate, so how can You tell me I must give thanks?'

Suddenly, it seemed that the starless, rainy night was the threshold of heaven. 'My son, angry men spat on Me, they beat Me, and then they nailed Me on to a cross to die because they hated Me. I know your pain and I grieve with you. But you must trust Me. I love you and I will never desert you. Just trust Me.'

All the fight seemed to drain out of Ali as he knelt by the side of the road. 'Oh Lord, You are so great. Forgive me for my arrogance. Help me to trust You no matter what the cost might be. I thank You for being so patient with me. And, I want You to know that no matter what happens to Silvana, I love You.'

17

The Valley of Death

The hospital room was dark and quiet, almost as if the shadow of death had come to visit and any light or sound would hasten it in its grim work. A shadow hovered over Silvana's face. Her eyes were sunken deep in their sockets and the skin on her face seemed like a thin wrapping of parchment stretched tightly across her cheek-bones. The pulse at her throat was visible.

Gentle sobs wracked the frame of her mother who was bent by the bedside. The door quietly opened and closed as Petros Silvanou stepped into the hall.

'Ali!' The words seemed torn from him. 'Ali, you have got to come and try to call her back. The doctor has done all he can, but it is almost as if she wants to die. Call her back for us.'

Ali staggered to his feet. Crying out to God for strength, he straightened his back and entered Silvana's room. Crossing over to her bed, he paused, shocked at the change in this girl who had once been so vibrant with life. A tear coursed its way down his cheek and fell unheeded to the floor. Bending down, he gently took her frail, cold hand in his and began to caress it. 'Silv, it's me, Ali. I've come to take you away. I love you, Silvana, and I need you. Please come back to me.'

That next hour seemed endless, as he struggled in vain to call her back from the valley of death. Her life seemed to be slipping right through his fingers. Pain welled up inside him, and he fell beside her bed. Losing control, he shouted her name again and again. With tears pouring down his cheeks, he laid his head in his arms and wept. Both Silvana's parents wept with him, knowing that their last hope had failed.

But far away, as though in a long tunnel, Silvana heard Ali's cries, calling her back. There was a feeble movement on the bed. Silvana's fingers moved painfully as though trying to reach out.

Silvana's mother gave a gasp as she saw her beloved daughter's eyes flutter open. 'Silvie, Silvie,' she cried with joy, 'you've come back to us.'

Lifting his head in wonder, Ali gazed into the eyes of his beloved. 'Silvie, my Silvie,' he whispered, as tears of joy filled his eyes.

'I'm thirsty. May I have a drink?' Her simple request brought laughter and a buzz of activity, as each bustled lovingly around her.

As the days passed, Silvana slowly gained strength. One afternoon, while she was sleeping, a huge bouquet of flowers arrived with a note. 'I am arranging for the wedding to take place in one month. *Mavramati.*'

The flowers were given to Mrs Silvanou, who set them in the corner of the room, careful lest she disturb her sleeping daughter. Looking at the card, she gasped in horror.

Hearing her daughter turning over, she quickly took the card and hid it in the folds of her dress.

'Mamma? What are you doing?' Silvana yawned.

'Some flowers arrived and I was just re-arranging them.'

'Who are they from? Is there a card?'

'No, I suppose the card must have been lost. I'm just going downstairs for a few minutes, my love.'

'All right.' Silvana stretched. 'Mamma?'

'Yes?' Her mother paused on the threshold.

'Will Daddy let Ali and me get married?'

A look of panic crossed her mother's face. Nervously, she laughed. 'Don't rush things, my dear. Besides, you are in no condition for marriage at the moment. Now close your eyes and try to rest.'

Obediently Silvana closed her eyes, but her thoughts were of Ali.

Her mother hurried down the stairs, out of the door, and caught a taxi to her husband's office. They had a hurried talk, and then she returned to the hospital.

The phone on Mavramati's desk rang. Flicking ash from his cigar, he picked up the phone. 'Mavramati here.'

'Hello. This is Mr Silvanou. I'm calling to thank you for the flowers you sent Silvana and . . .'

'Yes, well, they were a bit expensive but after all it's

only once in a lifetime you have to do that sort of thing. Now, I was thinking Friday would be a good day for the wedding. It fits in well with my work schedule.'

'I'm sorry, Mr Mavramati, but you don't understand. Silvana nearly died.'

'Understand? What is there to understand? She's on the mend now. That's all that matters.'

'Yes, sir, but I'm afraid she is not well enough to be married. She is still very weak and we haven't even told her that Melina died.'

'I don't know what all this has to do with me. I expect the wedding plans to go on as normal,' Mavramati sneered.

'I'm afraid that is impossible. The doctor has said she must have at least six months of quiet and rest without any stress . . .'

'Stress? I offer her a life of ease. There is no problem of stress, unless she is disobedient.'

'I am sorry, Mr Mavramati, but I must refuse to allow a marriage to occur at the moment. Perhaps in six months' time we can talk again.'

Before Mavramati could answer, Mr Silvanou had hung up his phone. He took out his handkerchief and wiped his face and his hands. The phone began to ring. Without a backward glance at the phone, he switched off the light and walked out of his office.

'Mamma, why doesn't Melina visit me? Is she all right?'

Silence hung over the room.

'Mamma, why won't anyone answer my questions?'

What happened that day?' Fear clutched at her heart and her hand went to her throat. 'She is dead, isn't she?' Silvana spoke calmly and very softly.

Startled, her mother answered. 'Yes, she is dead. I'm so sorry.'

'Sorry? What good is that? She is dead and I never even kissed her goodbye.' Silvana sat in stunned silence for a moment. Then a cry of anguish pierced the air.

'Melina, Melina!' Silvana began to wail loudly, rocking back and forth on her bed. 'Melina. Where was your God when you needed Him?'

During the next few days nothing could console Silvana. She became very bitter and in her anger refused to eat or care for herself. Once again, her strength began to ebb away.

One day, the door opened and a plump, middle-aged woman with short black curly hair and a kind face walked into the room. 'Silvana! It's me, Maria. You know, Melina's aunt.'

Sullenly Silvana looked up. 'Why did you come, and how can you smile when life is so cruel? Do you now worship the same God Melina did? What good did it do her? He never answered her prayers.'

'Oh Silvana, Silvana, your heart is becoming filled with hatred.' The older woman spoke gently as she enfolded the girl in her arms. 'God loves you so very much.'

'Fine way to show it, by taking my best friend away from me. It's not fair.'

'Silvana, stop it. Now listen to me. God does love you and He proved it by answering Melina's prayer for you.'

Silvana looked up, her eyebrows raised.

'She prayed that God would intervene so you wouldn't have to marry Mr Mavramati. You are still free, and there are rumours you may marry this boy you love. Is that true?'

The expression on Silvana's face lightened and a flicker of a smile creased her mouth. 'I don't know. Daddy did let Ali visit me.' The frown re-appeared. 'But what has that to do with Melina?'

'Has anyone told you what happened the day of your wedding?'

'No. No one speaks of it, though I do ask. It's as though they are afraid, though I don't know what could make me more upset than I am now.'

Maria seated herself comfortably on the bed and took Silvana's hand. Quietly she shared all that had happened that fateful day. Soon Silvana's eyes filled with tears.

Melina's aunt, tears streaming down her face, bravely continued: 'Melina's dying wish was that you be given this.' She drew a velvet parcel from her handbag and laid it in Silvana's hands. Sobs shook the slight form. She held the parcel to her and began to weep uncontrollably. The older woman gathered her in her arms and gently rocked her, like a mother comforting a small child.

18

Freedom

On his way to Mavramati's office, Petros Silvanou thought of the scene that had just met his eyes as he peeped into his daughter's hospital room. The sun had been shining through the window, and some of its rays had fallen on the mother and daughter, sitting on the bed. Seeing them in earnest conversation, he had felt a sense of gratitude that his child had been spared from the clutches of death. Thinking again of how close Silvana had come to death, he felt a rising surge of desire to protect her from further harm. A frown creased his brow, as he arrived at the scruffy building where Mavramati had his office.

'I'm sorry, Mr Silvanou, but it will be a few minutes before Mr Mavramati can see you,' said the secretary.

As she returned to her work, he paced up and down the reception area, waiting to be beckoned into the presence of his future son-in-law. He thought back to those threats that he could lose his home and his job at the catering company. He could almost feel his own sense of helplessness as he had allowed Mavramati to blackmail him. His brooding was broken into by the secretary, who announced that Mr Mavramati was ready to see him.

Stavros Mavramati stood by the window, which overlooked the busy street. 'Come in, come in, take a seat.'

Silvana's father sat down and stared across at the man who had caused him to compromise his life and family.

Stavros Mavramati spoke first. 'This is a big problem, what with this Muslim boy being involved with your daughter. However, I have decided to help her to take her mind off him.'

'You mean you still want to go through with the wedding?'

Stavros Mavramati looked piercingly at his proposed father-in-law. 'As I said, I will help her forget him.'

'Well, that is interesting, Mr Mavramati.' Petros stood up silently and raised his head almost in defiance, then spoke firmly. 'I have decided that this marriage is not right for my daughter. So, as of now, I am calling the whole thing off.'

Stavros Mavramati pressed both hands down on his desk, leaned forward, then said menacingly, 'I don't have to remind you about the house and catering factory, do I? You dare to call the wedding off and you will lose your home and your job. You are too old to get another secure livelihood.'

Petros Silvanou looked across the room, feeling the anger rising within him. 'Mr Mavramati, you slimy little creature, you can take my home and you can take my job. But know this, no longer will I be pushed around by your whims. You are not going to have my daughter!' Smashing his fist down upon the desk he continued: 'I am sick and tired of your threats and now *I* am going to do some threatening. Keep away from my family, or I will not only break all those horrible green teeth out of your face, but I will also leave you in little pieces all over this city!'

Silence descended on the room as a wave of fear swept over Stavros Mavramati. Petros straightened, and walked towards the door, then turned to look with scorn at the frightened man.

The door slammed with a tremendous thud which shook the room. Unsuspectingly, the secretary entered the room to be greeted with an angry shout. Stavros Mavramati sat alone, devastated by the knowledge that, for the first time in his life, he was unable to manipulate another through the use of fear.

Meanwhile, Silvana's mother had had to tell her daughter of Mavramati's approaches. The knowledge had once again deepened the gloom she felt. Even the room where she lay seemed to have darkened. Her mother sat beside her holding her hand. 'Oh Mamma, this tragedy never ends. It's like being in the death cell, going out for the hanging, and then having to postpone it for another week while they make the rope stronger.'

Just then her father walked into the room. Silvana froze for a moment as he bent over her and kissed her on the cheek.

He walked over to the door, closed it, then turned and faced his wife and daughter. 'I've seen Stavros Mavramati.' Just hearing the name made Silvana shudder.

'I've talked to him and to be honest, I've never felt better than I do now. I told him he can have his lousy job, he can take my home,' he paused, then smiled and spoke again softly while looking at Silvana, 'but he can't have my precious little daughter.'

His eyes filled with tears as he moved closer to the bed and, reaching out, he took Silvana into his arms. 'My child, I'm sorry I've caused you so much pain.' For minutes that seemed everlasting, the three held each other tightly; they were locked in an embrace of sweet love that seemed to flourish and blossom as, bathed in unashamed weeping, they found release for the months of pain.

The family sat together for a long time. Every so often Silvana reached out and squeezed her father's hand. This man, who had nearly sold her in a cowardly compromise, had now become her hero. 'I love you, Daddy,' she kept saying. They all laughed as he told of the look of horror on Stavros Mavramati's face when he had pounded on the desk.

After her parents had left, Silvana lay in her bed in the darkness. She smiled at the thought that she was truly free of Mavramati. Never again would she have to fear him. Like a bird suddenly free of its cage, her thoughts soared joyfully. Why, anything was possible now! Maybe she and Ali could even be married once she was released from the hospital.

Hospital! That word was like a black cloud spoiling her happiness.

'Melina,' she whispered. 'My dearest friend is dead. No! It cannot be. And yet, it happened here in this place. God chose to let me live and her die. Why? Melina was a good person. She deserved to live. Oh God, why did You let her die? Why?'

Sobs wracked her slight frame. 'Why, God? Why do You let evil people like Mavramati live, while You so casually snuff out the life of one so pure and gentle? Why, God? Melina loved You, but You didn't help her when she needed You. Why? Why?'

Holding the pillow cradled in her arms, she rocked back and forth sobbing, as the tears which had been locked away finally found release. Much later, she fell back, exhausted by her emotions, yet it was many hours before she finally fell into a restless sleep.

In the morning, Silvana refused to speak to the nurse as she bustled around the room, tidying the rumpled bed and helping Silvana to freshen up.

After the nurse had left the room, Silvana lay curled up in the corner of her bed, the tears silently stealing their way down her cheeks. From time to time she would raise her clenched fist, and weakly, futilely hit her pillow. When her breakfast arrived, she would not even turn to look at it, for the death of her beloved friend consumed her thoughts.

When the sun was shining full through the window, there was a gentle knock at the door. The door opened. There, as if she had been summoned, stood the one person Silvana felt would understand.

'Silvana, my dear. You have been crying. What is the matter?'

At the sound of concern in Maria's voice, the tears again began to flow. Immediately, the older woman sat on the bed, gathered Silvana into her arms and gently rocked the sobbing girl.

'There, there, my child. It's all right, go ahead and cry. That's right. It's not easy to lose your dearest friend.'

Maria's gentle acceptance comforted Silvana as she grieved, so that gradually she was able to put into words some of her anger and pain.

'Aunt Maria, Melina's death seems so senseless. She was so happy and so in love, and looking forward to her marriage to Costas. It just isn't fair. She had all her life before her. And now she's gone. Why? Why does God let so many cruel things happen? If He cares about people, why does He let them suffer? Why did He let Melina die?'

A shaft of sunlight fell across the bed bathing the two in an atmosphere of warmth and friendship. Maria looked down at her hands for a moment, seemed to gather together some inner strength, and then looked lovingly at the young girl.

'My dear, there are many things we will never understand. I do not know why God allowed Melina to die. I only know that God never makes a mistake, nor does He want to see us suffer.'

'Then why does He allow it?'

'There are many reasons. The truck driver had been drinking. The accident was the direct consequence of his sin. God gives us guidelines, but does not dictate how we must live. If we refuse to listen to His guidance, suffering often results. Many times innocent people are hurt. The devil is responsible for much suffering. His desire is to harm us; but the wonderful thing is that God is there to help us.

'I don't know why Melina had to die, Silvana. But I do know that God can use it for good in our lives, if we will only let Him.'

19

Answers

Petros Silvanou had an expression of new-found confidence upon his face. The experience of telling Stavros Mavramati exactly what he felt had released him from his former feelings of weakness. Even though he knew he was to receive his final wages in a few days because of his defiance, he felt content.

Unexpectedly, his boss, Mr Georgeou, called him into his office.

'Sit down, please. I have just received a long telephone call from Stavros Mavramati. He became a major shareholder in this company when my brother, Father Dimitri, who you probably know, sold out all his stock.

'Now, I don't know what you have done to Mavramati, but he is mad. Either I get rid of you or he says he will break up the company.' Mr Georgeou stood up angrily. 'Who does he think he is anyway – ? How long have you worked here?'

'Twenty-seven years, sir. I worked for your father

for ten years before his death.'

This made Mr Georgeou even more angry. 'Twenty-seven years, and he wants you fired just like that?' He picked up the telephone and asked his secretary to bring Silvanou's file into the office.

Petros sat very still, remembering the joy that he and his family had experienced the night before. Thoughts of the certainty of losing his job intruded. Somehow, though, Mr Georgeou seemed to be on his side. The file was handed to the angry businessman, who sat and browsed through it.

'You have never been late in twenty-seven years. In fact, your work record is excellent. Tell me, what is it that Mavramati has against you?'

Petros carefully recounted the story, showing no mercy on himself for his earlier compromise. Georgeou was visibly moved. 'Well, Petros, I don't want to make any promises, but I'll do what I can.'

'Thank you, sir.'

As the door closed after him, Georgeou got on the phone to his lawyer. 'Have the final papers gone through on the transfer of stock from my brother to Mavramati?'

'No,' was the tense reply.

'Good, tear them all up. Dimitri isn't selling. What would be the cost of a counter-suit for breach of contract?'

Georgeou sat back and whistled as the astronomical figure was quoted.

'All right, do what you can to stall while I talk to Dimitri.'

Quickly, the next call was put through. 'Dimitri, this is Nikos. You are not going to sell that stock to

Mavramati... What do you mean, you don't want to, but that you are in a difficult situation? Listen, Dimitri, I don't know what this character, Mavramati, has got on you, but listen to me carefully. I had arranged for you to keep the stock here to act as a security base for you when you are too old to play with your matchsticks. Now you get on the telephone and tell Mavramati the deal is off... I don't care if you *are* in a difficult situation – you need to live a little more like you preach.'

Georgeou put down the phone, then called his secretary to bring Petros Silvanou back into the office. As Petros entered the room, Georgeou spoke loudly. 'I'm a man of principle and I am not going to have some half-baked midget like Mavramati trying to blackmail me. You are going to stay with this company as long as I say and if...'

He was interrupted by the shrill sound of the telephone. He listened intently, nodding his head at intervals. 'Why didn't you catch this earlier?...It's in the fine print? Well, whatever, it serves our purposes perfectly. I will ring you later.'

He placed the phone down. 'Lawyers! You pay them the earth and they still mess things up.' He smiled, then stood up. 'Anyway, it's all sorted out.' He laughed as he spoke.

'My father, God rest his soul, was a man who understood people.'

Petros nodded in agreement.

'Well, he knew Dimitri was useless when it came to working or surviving in a business world. So he placed all his stock in a trust bond which could only be sold with either my consent or under my trusteeship. For the life of me, I cannot believe it has taken that useless lawyer ten years to discover that, but he insists it's legal. In other words, Dimitri can't sell his stock unless I agree to it.' He leaned forward, smiling but speaking through clenched teeth. 'I don't agree to it.'

Petros stood up and walked towards the door, turned, and said, 'Mr Georgeou, I can't ever thank you enough for what you have done.'

Georgeou smiled. 'Well, you can start by getting back out there and making me rich.' Both men were laughing as Petros closed the door.

In the days that followed, Melina's aunt, Maria, visited Silvana often, and they spoke much of Melina, of the accident and how Ali had given his blood so that she might live.

'Aunt Maria, Melina gave her life so that I could live. She was so happy and had so much to live for. Why did she do that when she knew I wanted to die rather than marry Mavramati?'

'Because she knew you weren't ready to die and she was.'

Silvana thought about this, frowning in bewilderment.

'How does one get ready to die?'

'Have you been reading Melina's New Testament?' asked Maria gently.

'Yes, I keep it close to me and read it often.'

'Look, here is a verse Melina loved. "It is by grace you have been saved, through faith – and this not from yourselves, it is the gift of God – not by works, so that no one can boast." Melina realised that she needed God as her friend and Saviour and asked Him to live His life in her. The Bible teaches that unless we come to God and receive the breath of His Spirit into our lives, we can never go to heaven.'

'But why not? If God is loving, why won't He take us to heaven?'

'Because He is holy and sin cannot enter His presence. It is only when the blood of Jesus washes the sins from our hearts that we can enter heaven.'

'But how could Jesus' blood...? Oh,' said Silvana, light dawning on her face, 'do you mean that when Jesus died, He gave His blood for me so that I could have spiritual life, just like Ali gave his blood so I could have physical life?'

'Exactly, my dear. Now you must rest. I will visit you tomorrow.' Maria kissed Silvana on both cheeks, gave her a hug and, smiling, left the room.

That night, Silvana tossed and turned in her bed. Her sleep was troubled by dreams of Melina's death. Finally, after waking, trembling with fear, she turned her lamp on and began to read Melina's New Testament. The thought of Melina dying for her caused her eyes to blur with tears and she began to weep. 'Oh Melina, I love you and yet I feel I'm rejecting your love by refusing to give my life to God. I'm afraid, so afraid!'

Sobbing, she began to pray, 'Oh God, help me. I feel so alone. Please breathe Your life into me.'

Lying down again, she fell into her first deep and restful sleep since she had learned of Melina's death.

20

Plans

Petros Silvanou sat down and stared across the room at the young man.

'Sir,' Ali spoke first, 'I have come here tonight to ask your forgiveness for causing so much trouble for your family. I am sorry.' He looked nervously at the carpet, then, gathering courage, looked directly into Silvana's father's eyes. 'But I want you to know I love your daughter.'

Petros jumped up. 'If your kind of love is a love that makes a girl be deceitful, then it's not much of a love.'

Ali sat and thought, then nodded his head. 'I know, and I am sorry. But we never acted in a way that would disgrace you when we were together.'

Silvana's father calmed down a little, and sat down. Ali took a deep breath.

'Sir, I want to ask your permission to marry Silvana.'

Petros turned away frowning, then said seriously,

'We are of different religions. It would be impossible to work that out without both you and Silvana experiencing that this is a hard, cruel world where people do unkind things to each other. What would your family say if you brought her home as your wife? No, it is impossible, you will just have to accept it.'

Ali felt as if his heart would break. Yet, deep within him, grew an awareness that God was in control and that he could relax in God's love. Unknowingly, he radiated a confidence that surprised Silvana's father.

Petros sat silent. He thought of Mr Georgeou and the mercy he had shown. Finally he nodded. 'When she leaves the hospital you can visit her here in my home. We can talk later about plans for the future.'

Ali left the house, very happy with the progress he had made. He was content to leave the rest to God. He began to attend a weekly Bible study with Costas. There were several young people who went, and the atmosphere was warm and friendly. Ali found himself growing in his faith in God.

Early in the new year, he felt an increasing desire to be baptised. Surely, baptism would have no link with orthodox Christianity, but rather would be a picture of the birth of his new life in God.

After much thought and prayer, he decided that in the spring, when the weather warmed up, he would be baptised in the river, declaring publicly his love for Christ.

21

The Uncles

The tea house was crowded as usual. Various elderly
men were playing backgammon with the effortless-
ness of masters. Others merely sipped tea and talked
about the old days and the present lack of respect
from the younger generation.

In the corner of the room was a television. An
American movie was blaring away, with girls dressed
immodestly. Everyone was complaining about how
irreligious and immoral the West was, yet everyone
kept watching, savouring each scene even as they
complained.

Ali's two uncles sat quietly in the corner drinking
tea from small glasses, while watching the television.
The elder, Mehmet, was tall, very powerful-looking,
with a hard face, which seemed to reflect a sharp
edge of hostility.

The younger brother, Ahmed, was smaller in build,
rather overweight, and generally less offensive in
appearance.

Mehmet was speaking forcefully. 'Once you allow compromise to set in, then who knows what will happen!' Ahmed nodded placidly in agreement. Mehmet continued, 'I knew there was something wrong when Selim left the village to make money wrestling. All this desire to read, write and understand; it only corrupts, you know. Now, look where it has led – to the pollution of his son! There's too much knowledge in the hands of people who don't know how to control it.'

He crumpled his empty cigarette box, threw it on the floor and trod on it. 'We should stamp it out before it goes any further.'

Ahmed nodded again, and they both turned to look with fascination at the immoral scenes on the television.

Silvana thought her heart would burst with joy. Her father, so moved by the events of the past months, had completely changed his mind and attitude. Ali had showed so much genuine concern, coming to the hospital every day, that her father had slowly begun to respect him.

The turning point for Petros had been the previous week, when he had gone to Mr Georgeou to seek his advice.

'Come in, come in. I'm busy, but let's talk.' Mr Georgeou seemed to live in two worlds; money-making at any cost, yet a genuine and human heart that was interested in people's emotions.

Petros Silvanou told his story, pouring out all the details without sparing himself any shame.

Mr Georgeou looked on; genuinely concerned, listening intently. He lit a cigarette. 'Religion! You would think that something that is supposed to be so closely linked with God would bring people together, rather than instilling even deeper prejudices. Look at my brother, Dimitri. He went to some monastery for six weeks, paid the right amount of money, and now he is a religious leader, even though his life stinks.' He shook his head and continued.

'It seems to me, from what you say, that these young people have more of a living religion in their lives than all the religious systems of their cultures and historical past. As to your family feuding; well, come on, face facts, they are going to feud anyway. You have a wedding, some uncle steals a bottle of whisky, you argue, then you don't talk for six months. Or some silly village wife has a dream and puts a curse on your cousin. It's all so petty. At least if you are persecuted for this, it is something worth suffering for.'

Petros listened intently as he went on. 'You make your own decision, but if it was me, I would tell these kids it's going to be hard, but so what? It's going to be hard anyway.'

Walking home, Silvana's father thought carefully over Mr Georgeou's words. He smiled as he thought of his illustration of an uncle stealing a bottle of whisky from a wedding. That's exactly what it is like, he thought. There are always arguments, always feuds over something.

He remembered his daughter's look of utter relief when he had come to the hospital to tell her that he had broken the engagement with Mavramati. The memory warmed his heart.

Perhaps it *was* possible to break the system of the centuries. Perhaps it *was* realistic to believe that love could triumph over hatred.

There were so many questions to be answered, yet somehow a resolution began to grow stronger in his heart; a resolution that he must let his daughter's love develop along its determined route. The difficulty was to know how to do it.

Ali and Silvana could not be married in the cathedral, as Ali was insistent that even though he now was a believer in Jesus, he was not a Christian in the orthodox sense of the word.

It was out of the question to be married by a Muslim *imam*, as Silvana was not a Muslim and anyway, a move like that could create a riot in the town.

Petros was aware that all his relatives were opposed to such a friendship being allowed to develop, as were Ali's family. Indeed, as Ali continued to visit the Silvanou home, gossip was already starting to grow, as relatives and neighbours were scandalised by their behaviour.

He shook his head as he drew near to his house. It was such a complex situation; yet, somehow, the answer must be found.

Aysha was just coming into the house when Silvana came rushing towards her and threw her arms around her.

'Oh Aysha, I'm so excited! My father has agreed that Ali and I can be married.'

Aysha's face lit up with joy. 'Oh Silv, I'm so happy for you.' They went into the living-room and sat down. The sun poured through the window, causing everything in the room to be bathed with light.

'Silvana, what happened?'

'Ali came to see my father last night. After a while, they both came in here, smiling. Dad put his arm around me and said, "Well, when do you think is a good time for a wedding?"'

'Tell me about the wedding. When and where is it going to be?'

'I don't know. We somehow have to do things in a way that won't offend everybody.'

Silvana glanced up. A shadow crossed her face as she saw Melina's picture on the far wall. She looked down at the carpet, her eyes filling with tears. 'How I wish Melina could have been here!'

Wiping the tears away, she turned to her visitor. 'Thank you for being my friend, Aysha. No one could ever take Melina's place and yet you have given so much to me. I do appreciate you.'

Aysha smiled, then reached out and held Silvana's hand.

22

Mehmet's Revenge

It was February and there was a chill in the air. Ali had spent the morning with Costas, and as he walked up the street towards the house where he lived, he saw a figure pacing nervously up and down.

'Dad!' Ali called, and hurried forward. His father turned and waited, almost as though he dreaded the coming encounter.

'Dad. It's great to see you!' The two embraced, greeting each other with the traditional kiss on each cheek.

Once inside, Ali made tea and the two sat chatting about the family. After a few minutes his father stood up, coughed, and looked very serious.

'Ali, you must give up this new religion. That unclean Christian girl who you say you love has influenced you to reject your family.'

'Father, I am not an orthodox Christian,' said Ali patiently. 'I am a believer in Jesus and I can never deny Him. I have not changed religions. One night I had a dream and it told me Jesus was the way to God. I have met God.'

'Stop this, Ali. Don't you see that you are bringing great shame on your family? By doing this, you are turning your back on your culture, your history, and even on your family. You shame me and you will be the death of your mother. She sits weeping for her beloved son.' Ali's father paused, cleared his throat, then spoke with great emotion. 'Come home to us and forget this nonsense.'

Ali responded gently. 'Father, I love you and my mother. I always will. My first son will bear your name. He will be circumcised, will do his military service, will honour his history and his prophets. He will dress as you and I dress. He will eat our food, prepared our way. He will pray kneeling on the ground with his hands raised towards heaven, but he will also learn about Jesus. He will learn about a God of love, and I will teach him to reject superstitions that are not found in any Holy Book, but rather are made up by old men and women in the villages.'

His father looked moved. It was difficult for him to understand Ali's attitude, which was different from what his brothers had warned him about.

Ali continued strongly, 'You never complain if men go to the brothel, or if some of your relatives drink alcohol. You never say a word about your cousins who don't keep the fast. Our family has never talked about going on the pilgrimage and yet, now, suddenly everyone has become fanatical and is talking about me as if I was an infidel, rejecting my family and its ways.'

Ali's father stood astonished at his son's wisdom.

'And what religion will you put on your children's identification cards?'

Ali looked up at his father, then down at the floor. 'That I don't know.'

Ali's father turned and slowly walked through the door, as if in a trance. Ali, deeply moved, fell on his knees to pray for his family.

The day was slow in coming, and fog hung like a curtain blocking out the sunlight. As Ali woke, he felt a chill go through his bones and snuggled deeper under his covers. Then, opening his Bible, he read a verse from the Psalms: 'Precious in God's sight is the death of His beloved children.'

'That is a strange verse. Why should our death . . . *my* death, be special to You, God?' Sitting quietly for a few moments, looking out at the fog, he smiled. 'Of course! If I die, the fog is lifted and I can see the face of God clearly. That is special to You too, Father God, for You love me and desire my presence with You. Lord, help me be ready for that day when You call me home.'

In another house, in a village some distance away, smoke curled from the chimney as Ali's uncle Mehmet rose from his bed. Bitterness filled his heart. The thought of what Ali's father had told him of Ali's quiet statement of faith in God angered him. How could Ali dare say he had met God – that God now lived in his heart, having cleansed him from sin? No man could say such things! It must be the evil influence of those Christians he had met at university. And now there were rumours that he was talking about baptism. Things had gone too far and must be stopped!

Thinking these thoughts, Mehmet moved instinctively towards a cupboard. Unlocking a drawer, he drew out a cloth bundle. In the bundle, carefully wrapped, was a gun. After looking it over carefully, he began to clean it. Bitter thoughts of revenge on Christian infidels were surging through his mind. Putting the gun in his pocket, he picked up his jacket and moved to the door.

His wife turned around anxiously. 'Mehmet, where are you going?'

'To do the work of Allah, woman!' he responded harshly as he slammed the door and disappeared into the mist.

Several hours later, as Ali was working in the factory, his boss appeared. 'There is a man to see you. Says he is your uncle and that it is urgent. You may take your lunch break now.'

Ali walked thoughtfully down the hall to the lobby where his uncle waited.

'Hello, Uncle. What brings you here? Is . . .?'

'Don't call me Uncle.' The words were spoken with deep hatred. 'I have come to warn you of the error of your ways.'

Calmly, Ali said, 'Why don't we go outside and talk this over?' He laid his hand on his uncle's arm, as if to pacify him.

Mehmet brushed off the hand with disgust. 'Don't touch me! You are a Muslim and I intend to see that you remain a Muslim, even if it means your death.'

'Uncle, I love God. He is my Friend. He gave His life for me, and I will love Him no matter what the cost may be.'

'Do not speak pious words to me, you traitor!' Mehmet spoke venomously, drawing the gun out of his pocket. 'I will see that you turn from the Christian God.'

Ali stood straight and tall. 'There is only one God and He loves every human being. To Him, there is no religion which can reach Him. His way is for us to humble ourselves and to acknowledge our need for forgiveness from sin. He loves you, Uncle, and He died so that you could live.'

Mehmet's face had turned a livid red as Ali spoke. Losing control of himself, he screamed in Ali's face, 'allah is great!' Then he pulled the trigger of the gun and emptied the pistol into the body of his nephew.

Ali staggered backward, stretching out his hand to his uncle and then looking towards heaven. 'Father, forgive him!' he implored, and fell face down on the ground. 'Uncle, I forgive you,' he gasped, his hand still stretched out to his uncle as it went limp.

Chaos broke out, as workers who had come to see what the noise meant began to run about in fear. In the confusion, Mehmet slipped out of the door and raced away through the streets.

Silvana lay on her bed, numb with disbelief. Questions filled her mind. 'How can God be so cruel? Why did He let Ali die just when we were going to find happiness together?'

Could it really be true that Ali was no more? That

the warm, loving face she loved so much would never smile at her again?

The thought of jumping out of the window and joining him in death was a real option. There was no reason for living.

Ali was gone and, with his death, all hope had died within her. How could a God who professed to be loving allow such overwhelming tragedy to fill her life? First Melina, who was like a beloved sister, had died, and now there was the cruel and senseless death of Ali. It was more than she could bear.

That afternoon Costas visited the Silvanou home. While waiting for Aysha to bring Silvana into the room, he looked at the photograph of Melina. How could one small circle of friends know so much tragedy in such a short time?

The door opened and Aysha led Silvana into the room. Collapsing on to the chair, she sat limp and forlorn. 'Costas? Why, when everything was working out so well, did God allow this to happen?'

Slowly Costas shook his head with bewilderment. 'I just don't know, Silvana. I don't have any answers. All I can say is that it is a very confused and untidy world where prejudice and hatred are so strong. God is not taken by surprise by this tragedy, even though we are. Perhaps He wants to use people like the three of us to influence our world for good, by walking the path of love and forgiveness in spite of our pain.'

The sun shone through the window and children could be heard playing outside in the street. The clock ticked softly in the background as the three friends sat silently, united in a bond of love and mourning.

23

Beyond the Grave

Mehmet had been caught and put into prison. After being badly beaten, he had been put under special security.

Ali's brother Hassan had made a vow outside the mosque, loudly declaring that he would avenge his brother's death. There were rumours that his brother had become a Christian. Hassan angrily refuted these, saying that his uncle had made up some malicious lies to cover his real reason for murdering Ali. Hassan then spread a new rumour that his uncle's real motive had been that a fortune-teller had told him that if Ali was not murdered soon, all his own family would die within the month.

Two days after Ali's death, many of the villagers gathered at the mosque for the funeral. The day was bitterly cold, with a harsh north wind blowing. Many had come out of curiosity, joining the weeping relatives and friends. As the coffin was brought out of the mosque, Ali's mother let out an unearthly

shriek and then, wailing loudly, began to beat her
breast in her deep grief. The other women joined in
the wailing, and slowly the group followed the coffin
to the graveyard.

Costas slipped into the rear of the procession along
with several young people from the Bible study group
that Ali had attended. Silvana had come with them,
her head covered modestly with a black scarf she had
then wrapped around her face so that only her tearstained eyes showed.

The coffin was placed on the ground, and the lid
was opened. At the sight of Ali's lifeless form, the
wailing seemed to grow even louder. His mother fell
on to her knees by the coffin, and, laying her head on
her son's chest, began to weep inconsolably. After
some minutes, Ali's father pulled her away.

The *hodja* read and chanted some prayers, then
left, leaving the anguished mourners by the coffin.
Each person then went up to the casket and, taking a
handful of earth, dropped it into the coffin as they
passed. Most sobbed brokenly as despair filled their
hearts.

Then everyone just stood, as though uncertain of
what to do next. In this hesitation, the group of
young people silently knelt around the coffin, their
heads bowed and tears streaming down their cheeks.

Quietly Silvana whispered, 'Goodbye, my beloved.
One day we will meet in heaven where we will never
be parted.'

Shyly Costas raised his head towards heaven and
in the hush that followed, prayed reverently, 'Oh
God, we give Ali back to You. Each of us loved him.
Thank You that now he is in heaven with You.

'Comfort those who remain behind and especially be close to his family, that they may know You love them.

'Thank You that Your love never changes, and help each of us to find you, even as Ali did, so that one day we may be reunited with him in heaven. Amen.'

Everyone in the crowd was weeping quietly.

Gently, the men of the family placed the lid on the coffin and let it down into the ground. Then they and Ali's close friends helped to cover it with earth.

Each shovelful of earth seemed to make Ali's death more final. The weeping continued. But, whereas before all had been total despair, now a feeling of hope began to take root. Perhaps this was not the final parting after all.

24
Silvana's Gift

After hearing of Ali's death, Costas and Petros Silvanou had gone to the house where he had been boarding. They gathered together his belongings. Knowing that Ali's father would be afraid of his Bible, they had given it to Silvana, and had taken the rest of his things to his parents.

Several months later, as Silvana sat holding Ali's Bible, she remembered how she had also received Melina's Bible. Having that was like having a part of Melina. Also, as she had read the words of that Holy Book, she had found hope and courage to go on living.

With determination she rose and carefully wrapped Ali's Bible in some cloth. Then, hurrying downstairs, she spoke with her mother, telling her of her plans.

'Silvana, I don't think that is wise. She might harm you, even put a curse on you.'

'It's all right, Mother. Jesus will protect me.'

'Well, wear your scarf and have your face covered as you walk through the village.'

'Yes, Mother. Don't worry. I can spend the night with Aysha and be back tomorrow afternoon.'

Wearing a light cape to protect her against the chill of the early spring morning, Silvana set off for the bus station.

As the bus neared its destination, Silvana's face turned pale with fear; her hands became cold and clammy. Perhaps it had been a foolish idea after all. She could just sit at the station and catch the first bus home. No one would blame her if she was unable to make the visit.

'Oh, God. Please help me! I'm so afraid. Give me strength to do what is right without fear of what the cost will be.'

As the bus pulled to a stop and opened its doors, Silvana checked to make sure her scarf was properly in place. Then, clutching her parcel to her, she slowly walked down the aisle and off the bus. Several times she headed down the wrong street before she finally arrived at Aysha's house. The sun was shining, the birds singing and the air fresh with the promise of spring, so she did not mind the detours.

As Aysha opened the door, she stared in surprise. 'Silvana! What are you doing here?'

'I've come to visit Ali's mother.'

Stunned, Aysha drew Silvana into the house. 'Let's have a glass of tea and we can talk.'

Seated with tea and fruit on the table, Aysha frowned as she stirred the sugar in her glass.

'Silvana, do you really think it is wise?'

'I know what you're thinking, Aysha, and you're probably right. But Ali's mother should have his Bible. I'm sure she will draw comfort from it. What I was wondering was if you would come with me to show me the way. You could wait down the road so she won't get angry with you.'

'Of course I'll go with you – all the way to the house.'

Silvana drew a deep breath. 'Thank you. I will feel much stronger if you are with me.'

The two girls then bowed in prayer, asking God to surround Ali's mother with His love.

Quietly they set off, walking down the lane. Rounding the bend, they saw a wooden house sitting at the top of the hill.

'This is it, Silvana. Are you quite sure you want to go through with it?'

Silently Silvana nodded and then began the climb to the house, Aysha following her closely.

Arriving at the door, Silvana hesitated, bit her lip, and then knocked on the door. There was the sound of footsteps on the wooden floor and then the door swung open, revealing a short, squat figure clothed in a black cotton dress, with a black apron, heavy black stockings, and her hair covered by a black scarf.

'Aysha, come in. It's good to see you.' A faint smile crossed Ali's mother's face as she embraced her niece and they kissed each other on each cheek.

'Aunt Fatima, I've brought someone to see you.'

Silvana slipped off her scarf and smiled gently at Ali's mother.

'Hello. I am Silvana, the girl Ali wanted to marry.'

The older woman's eyes blazed with anger. Speaking to Aysha, yet not taking her eyes off Silvana, she said bitterly, 'Get that filthy girl out of my house. If it wasn't for her, my son would still be alive.'

'I understand how you feel, but I had to see you,' Silvana answered.

Very calmly and deliberately Fatima spat in Silvana's face. 'I hate you!' she shouted.

Using her scarf, Silvana wiped her face. 'I love you and I forgive you.'

'Forgive? You have nothing to forgive. You deserve much worse.' Trembling with anger, she spat again.

As the saliva ran down Silvana's cheek, she smiled. 'Ali's blood runs in my veins. Because of this your life and my life are now linked. I am glad.'

Startled, Fatima raised her eyebrows. 'What do you mean?'

'When I lay dying in the hospital, the doctor put a needle in Ali's arm and then attached that to a needle in my arm. His blood flowed through the tubing and into my body. I am alive today because he gave his blood for me. Because of that, I feel as if there is a bond between you and me.'

Fatima had expected Silvana to be both frightened and insulted, yet instead the girl spoke calmly of love as though she were not in the least afraid. Confused by her response, she remained silent.

'I have brought you something . . .'

'I want nothing from you. Now leave my house or I will have a curse put on you,' snapped Fatima, her voice raised in anger. Silvana took no notice.

'This belonged to Ali. I kept it because of my love for him. Whenever I have held this in my hands I have felt a closeness to him. You see, it was more than love that held us together. Ali was searching for God. After my accident, we each came to realise that

Jesus had given His blood so that we might live – just as Ali gave his blood for me. This is the book he loved so dearly. I want you to have it because it was so precious to your son. I am praying it will help bring comfort to your heart.' Silvana held out the book, still wrapped in its cloth.

Fatima was stunned. From the moment Silvana had walked through her door, it was as if things had gone beyond her realm of understanding. To have this girl, whom she hated so viciously, standing fearlessly in front of her and responding in love was itself like a dream; but to be offered her son's Holy Book when she herself had been so full of hate was overwhelming.

Falteringly, she took the Bible and turned silently away, holding the book to her heart.

'May God bless you and enfold you in His love,' Silvana said gently, and then left the house.

Aysha walked over to her aunt and kissed her. 'Goodbye, Auntie. I'll be in to see you tomorrow.'

Numbly, Fatima nodded her head.

As the door closed behind the girls, Fatima's body began to tremble. Slowly she walked over to the stool by the fire and, seating herself, began to rock back and forth, holding the book close to her body as though it were a baby. For a while, tears stole silently down her wrinkled cheeks and then, as her body began to shake with sobs, she put her apron over her head and wailed out her anguish, grief and broken dreams.

As the girls walked back down the hill to Aysha's home, they were both silent, wrapped in their own thoughts of Ali, of his death, and of his mother.

Arriving at Aysha's home, they collapsed on the sofa. Silvana closed her eyes, leaning back against the cushions, as the tears began to fall.

'You were very brave,' said Aysha reassuringly.

'Not really. I was terrified until I actually saw her. Seeing the deep grief and hopelessness in her eyes made me forget myself. I just longed to comfort her.'

'Although she didn't show it, I know she was touched by your gift.'

'Perhaps. I just wish we could become friends, though I realise that would be very difficult for her, what with her being Muslim and me being Christian. You know, Aysha, Ali used to say to me that being born a Christian wouldn't help me with God. He said we were confused by labels, and what really mattered was to get to know God personally. I would laugh and tell him not to be so serious. When he died, I realised that I couldn't face life just as a Christian – that I needed more. That more – well, it was to become God's own child by accepting His love and sacrifice for me.'

'I know what you mean. Being God's own child is very special. It's what gives hope to life when everything seems so bleak.' Aysha spoke gently, for she sensed that Silvana still felt discouraged.

'Aysha, let's pray that Ali's mother might come to realise that God has reached down in love to us. That we don't have to earn His favour.'

Aysha smiled at her friend. 'Ali once told me that he was praying for both you and his family. He said he would be willing to face anything if you and his family would only come to know God personally. I think your prayers will make him very happy.'

25

The Promise of Spring

It was a typical crisp March day, with stong winds blowing through every corner, tugging at the trees, and whistling down the chimneys. Silvana sat in the living-room, gloomily staring into the fire that danced to the whims of the wind.

There was a knock at the door, which she ignored, not feeling up to entertaining some chatty visitor. The knocks persisted and finally, in exasperation, she rose and walked slowly to the door, still hoping the unwanted visitor would leave.

To her amazement, when she opened the door, she found Aysha on her doorstep. 'Aysha! What are you doing here?'

'I was just getting ready to give up and let the wind carry me back to the bus station,' she replied, laughing. 'I'm so glad that you are home.'

'Oh, dear. You look so cold. Come in and get warmed by the fire.'

Laughing, the girls hugged and then went into the living-room.

Aysha went up to the fire and held her hands out to warm them. 'Hmm. This feels lovely.'

'Let me get you a drink.' Silvana hurried to the kitchen and was soon back with a tray of cake, fruit, and steaming glasses of tea.

After chatting casually, Silvana frowned. 'What ever brought you to the city? You look like the cat who stole the cream! What has happened?'

'I was so excited, I just had to see you. I know it was hard for you to part with Ali's Bible and even harder to face his mother. I really admired you for the way you took Aunt Fatima's behaviour. Yet I sensed you felt discouraged.'

'I did. In fact, I still am. For all I know my idea may have been totally wrong. Why, she might have been so angry with me that she destroyed Ali's Bible.'

Aysha smiled. 'But you see, she hasn't! After you left, it started to rain and it rained for three days. The fourth day it tapered off, so I thought I'd go to see Aunt Fatima. Sloshing through the mud, I wondered about how I would be able to find out what she had done with the Bible.'

'What did you do? Did you see it? Was she angry?' Silvana asked apprehensively.

Aysha laughed. 'One question at a time. Well, I knocked, and as no one answered, I knocked louder. I thought I heard a sob so I opened the door and stepped inside. Aunt Fatima was on her stool in front of the fire. She was rocking back and forth, hugging the Bible to herself, and softly moaning, the tears streaming down her cheeks. I went up to her and kissed her. Still looking into the fire, she started talking about Ali. After a while, she looked at me for the first time and said, "I have been reading Ali's Holy Book. At first, I just held it, but then I felt if I opened it, maybe I could understand what happened to Ali. He was always a thoughtful boy. Why would he go against all he had been taught?

'"All my life, I have wondered about how I could please God, yet He has always seemed so distant. Reading Ali's Book fills me with questions, but it also brings me peace. I am so grateful to your friend for bringing it to me."'

Silvana's mouth fell open. 'Did she really say that?'

'Yes. Isn't it exciting?'

'Oh, Aysha, I'm so happy!' Silvana jumped off the couch and twirled around the room. Her eyes sparkled with joy, then suddenly filled with tears.

'Ali loved his family and longed for them to really know God. He was always praying for them.'

Aysha nodded and then spoke thoughtfully. 'One day beauty is going to come out of his death. We may not understand all the whys and wherefores now, but spring always follows the winter. God is able to bring life even out of the midst of death.'

With hope springing up in their hearts, the two girls hugged.

From the Authors

Dear Friend,

For most of us, life has moments of pain and suffering. Often we find ourselves in situations where we wonder, 'Why has this happened to me?'

Unhappy events do not come from the hand of an angry God. It is true that He allows pain in our lives – but in the midst of that pain, He offers Himself. God loves you very much. He understands what you are going through and He is greater than your circumstances. In fact, He longs to give you joy in the midst of your pain.

We would be happy to hear from you.

In His love,
Bob & Barbara

PO Box 17
Bromley
Kent
England